Of Nightingales That Weep

By Katherine Paterson

Of Nightingales That Weep

Illustrated by Haru Wells

AN AVON CAMELOT BOOK

Grateful acknowledgment is made to George Allen and Unwin Ltd. and to Grove Press Inc., for permission to reprint lines from the Nō play, "Ikuta," by Zembo Motoyasu. Translated by Arthur Waley in *The Nō Plays of Japan*. New York: Grove Press, Inc., 1957.

AVON BOOKS
A division of
The Hearst Corporation
1790 Broadway
New York, New York, 10019

First Camelot Printing, September 1980

The T.Y. Crowell edition carries the following Library of Congress
Cataloging in Publication Data:
    SUMMARY: The vain young daughter of a samurai finds
    her comfortable life ripped apart when opposing warrior
    clans begin a struggle for imperial control of Japan.
        1. Japan—History—Gempei Wars, 1180-1185—Juv.
    fiction. [1. Japan—History—Gempei Wars, 1180-1185—
    Fiction] 1. Wells, Haru, illus. II. Title.

Printed in the U.S.A.

OP 10 9 8 7 6 5

For
Elizabeth PoLin Paterson
with love

KATHERINE PATERSON is the Newbery Award-Winning author of *Jacob Have I Loved* and *Bridge to Terabithia* and the two-time National Book Award Winner for *The Master Puppeteer* and *The Great Gilly Hopkins*. Mrs. Paterson was born in China and spent part of her childhood there. She also lived, studied and taught in Japan. Her four children and their friends have provided her with some of the subject matter for her sharply observant stories of family life. Katherine Paterson lives with her husband and four children in Norfolk, Virginia.

Contents

Pronunciation of Japanese Names

Generally speaking, if you pronounce the consonants the way you would expect to in English, you'll get close to a recognizable Japanese pronunciation for most of them. In words that appear to have diphthongs, like Heike, the two vowel sounds are both pronounced, though to the unpracticed ear they seem like a single sound. A long vowel, like ō, is simply a drawing out of the regular vowel. Thus in the word, Kyōto, count two beats on the first o.

    a = *ah*, as in f*a*ther
    e = *e*, as in l*e*g
    i = *ee*, as in s*ee*
    o = *o*, as in s*o*
    u = *u*, as in fl*ue* or t*oo* (but keep sound short)

Thus we have:

Takiko	Tah-kee-koh
Goro	Goh-roh
Chieko	Chee-eh-koh
Fusa	Foo-sah
Kiyomori	Kee-yoh-moh-ree
Heike	Heh-ee-keh (Hay-keh)
Genji	Gehn-jee
Kenreimon'in	Kehn-reh-ee-mohn-een (Ken-ray-mon-een)
Chujo	Choo-joh (In this name both vowels are long)
Munemori	Moo-neh-moh-ree
Yoshitsune	Yoh-shee-tzoo-neh

A Historical Note

The political situation existing in Japan during the Gempei War (1180–1185), at the time this book takes place, was unstable — to say the very least. For many years the Emperor had been a mere figurehead, and the real power of the nation had resided in a noble family or clan called Fujiwara. By the twelfth century the fortunes of the Fujiwaras had waned, and a struggle for ascendancy developed between two warrior clans, the Heike, also called the Taira, and the Genji, also called the Minamoto. This intense rivalry came to its first climax during the Hogen Insurrection (1156–1159), which found the two clans supporting opposing elements within the Imperial household. The Heike, led by Kiyomori, triumphed, and for the rest of Kiyomori's life he was, in effect, the ruler of Japan. However, he was never completely at ease in his position, and one of those who remained a thorn in his flesh was Go Shirakawa, who had retired as Emperor in 1158 but who continued to wield a great deal of influence.

Here is a brief Who's Who of the chief historical figures of the period.

From the Heike Clan

LORD KIYOMORI (1118–1181). The most famous and powerful of the Heike. He rose to power over the nation after the Hogen Insurrection, in which he supported the cause of Go Shirakawa against rival Imperial factions supported by Yoshitomo of the Genji.

LADY KIYOMORI (d. 1185). Also called Nii no Ama, she became a nun after her husband's death, but apparently remained a prominent figure at court.

MUNEMORI (d. 1185). He succeeded his father as chief of the Heike and was commander during the Gempei War.

TOKUKO. The daughter of Kiyomori, she married Emperor Takakura and became Empress Kenreimon'in. She was the mother of Emperor Antoku and one other son, whose name is not known.

From the Genji Clan

YORITOMO (1147–1199). He was the eldest of three sons born to Yoshitomo of the Genji by a favorite mistress. After the defeat and death of his father and older half brothers, Yoritomo took upon himself the re-forming of his clan to exact vengeance on the Heike.

NORIYORI (d. 1193). He is the second of the three brothers and joined Yoritomo in his efforts against the Heike.

YOSHITSUNE (1159–1189). Though the youngest of Yoshitomo's sons and the one whom his father probably never saw, Yoshitsune of the Genji emerges as the most romantic and tragic hero of Japanese history. He was un-

doubtedly a brilliant commander, so brilliant that despite
all he accomplished for the Genji cause, his brother
Yoritomo came to fear him and plotted to destroy him.

YOSHINAKA (1154–1184). A cousin of the three brothers
and an ally until he met Go Shirakawa, who brought his
death at their hands.

From the Imperial Family

Go SHIRAKAWA, Senior Cloistered Emperor (1127–1192).
He became Emperor at the age of twenty-eight, but he retired in three years and was replaced by his son Nijo.
When Nijo died in 1165, he in turn was succeeded by his
infant son Rokujo. After several years Go Shirakawa was
able to effect the retirement of Rokujo and replace him
with his favorite son, Takakura. (The custom of an Emperor abdicating or retiring at an early age was firmly
entrenched by this time in Japanese history. The idea
was, perhaps, that the younger the Emperor, the more
malleable.) Shirakawa saw two more Emperors come to
the throne and a complete change of power from the
Heike to the Genji clan.

TAKAKURA, Retired Emperor (1161–1181). The son of Go
Shirakawa by a kinswoman of Kiyomori, he became Emperor at seven and abdicated in favor of his son, Antoku,
when he was nineteen. Never strong physically, he died
the next year.

ANTOKU, Emperor (1178–1185). On the one side he had
the wily Retired Emperor Go Shirakawa for a grandfather, and on the other Kiyomori, the bear of the Heike.
He himself was not able to survive the power struggles
that surrounded his life.

And lightly he ran,
Plucked at the warrior's sleeve,
And though his tears might seem like the long woe
Of nightingales that weep,
Yet were they tears of meeting-joy,
Of happiness too great for human heart.
So think we, yet oh that we might change
This fragile dream of joy
Into the lasting love of waking life!

—ZEMBO MOTOYASU

Of Nightingales That Weep

ONE

The Daughter of Lord Moriyuki

The daughter of a samurai does not scream when her hair is being combed. Indeed, she makes no sound at all. It was one of the more elementary rules of conduct that her mother had drummed into her for eleven years. Nonetheless, when Choko yanked the comb through a particularly stubborn knot, Takiko, daughter of Lord Moriyuki of the Heike clan, cried out. "Choko! You're trying to kill me!"

"Nonsense!" snapped the maid. "Just hold still, and it won't pull so much." She gave another sound yank. "Where were you yesterday? Your hair looks as if crows had been nesting in it."

"*Aeii!* Stop it. I'll tell my aunt on you. You have no respect."

· 1 ·

The maid proved unmoved by her threat. "Will you also tell her where you were hiding when it was time for your koto lesson?" she asked mildly, lifting a hank of long black hair up to the light as if to show up the tangles. Then she sank in the comb and jerked it, like a knife, through the heart of the snarl.

Takiko was nearly pulled off her knees, but this time she bit her lip. She mustn't give Choko the satisfaction of another protest. "Stupid Choko," she thought. "Servants are all stupid." None of them could understand why she hid. They probably thought it was because she hated music.

Her concentration shifted from the pain in her scalp to the contemplation of her secret.

She smiled inwardly. If the rest of the household only knew. She could remember vividly the day that the truth had occurred to her. The rain was beating against the wooden shutters. In the dim lamplight, Aunt was pressing Takiko's small fingers down upon the strings and guiding her right hand as the plectrums attached to her fingers plucked the strings of the koto. Suddenly she knew. There was no music inside her aunt, who was breathing on her neck and singing the Chinese song in a harsh, aged voice. No. The music was inside her—Takiko. She was not simply a samurai's daughter who had to be forced to learn the arts of entertainment befitting her station; *she was a maker of music*.

From that day, nearly a year ago, she could hardly bear to take direction from her aunt, for Lady Uchinaka's playing was square and precise, like the earnest brushstrokes of a rather clever beginner, while the music within Takiko danced like the sweeping calligraphy of a master artist. She knew this. But she could not explain it to anyone, because the music within her head had not yet reached her fingertips. If she tried to talk about it, she might be scolded for her arrogance, or worse yet, she might be laughed at.

"That's better," Choko was saying. "Now you're behaving more like the daughter of a samurai."

Takiko listened carefully for the hidden laughter. Choko's tone appeared ordinary, but servants had so many ways of sneering. Everyone had pretended to be impressed when Lord Kiyomori — Prime Minister, military commander of the nation, grandfather and protector of the infant Emperor, and chief of the Heike clan — had summoned her father to his presence: "What an honor! Lord Kiyomori has never forgotten our Lord Moriyuki's brilliance and courage during the uprisings twenty years ago!" "When the Genji clan threaten, doesn't Lord Kiyomori always call first upon Lord Moriyuki?" "Yes, yes. Lord Moriyuki is the sword in our commander's hand." They had bubbled on like sulphur springs; and she like a foolish child had been so proud.

But yesterday, as she lay hidden in the shed behind the garden, she had heard their true thoughts: "Why on earth would Lord Kiyomori send for *him*? He's like an old turnip pickled for twenty years in a barrel of rice wine." Takiko had been unable to recognize the voice, muffled as it was by the wall of the shed. But she had heard the laughter, no longer hidden, that greeted the remark. It had washed over her like something filthy.

"There," said Choko, resting back on her heels. "You are almost presentable again. Your father is waiting to see you."

"My father's back? Why didn't you tell me?"

"You could hardly have gone to him looking the way you did this morning."

Takiko jumped to her feet.

"Don't run," Choko warned. "It isn't proper."

Takiko gave an impatient *ummph* and slowed her step, not for Choko's sake, for her father's.

Lord Moriyuki was sitting cross-legged before a small table. There was a lacquer wine cup on the table, but he seemed to be ignoring it. She could never remember seeing him look quite so noble before. His hair was bound neatly into a samurai topknot, and he was wearing a blue silk blouse with great full trousers of deep green. Takiko's mother was kneeling, eyes downcast, in a far corner of the room. It was an important occasion. Takiko bowed her head to the matting and murmured a formal greeting which she had once heard her aunt give to an uncle of the Emperor.

"What a pretty child," her father said. "And such lovely manners. She'll make a brilliant marriage, Chieko. Though I may not live to see it."

Takiko brought her forehead off the mat. It was even more serious than she had first thought. Her father only used that tone of voice for state funerals.

"I have come home to say farewell, my child. There is rebellion fomenting in the north." His voice was rich, his grammar elegant. The child watched him, her chest filling with pride. He paused and took a sip from the cup before him. His eyes closed as he savored it. He cleared his throat and continued. "Our Lord Kiyomori has chosen us to put the traitors to the sword."

"Oh, Father! How wonderful!"

Something like a sob came from the direction of her mother. Takiko turned to her, puzzled. Her father also turned his head.

"Woman, you are the daughter and the wife of samurai."

Chieko put a small pale hand across her mouth.

"You must care for your mother in my absence, Takiko."

"Yes, Father."

"Remember all your aunt's kindnesses"—he chose the words carefully—"in our less fortunate days and obey her."

"Yes, Father."

"Practice your koto as she directs."

Takiko's eyes went to the mat floor. "Yes, Father."

"My daughter will make a good marriage, Chieko. Has Lady Uchinaka made inquiries at court as I requested?"

"My lord, Takiko is only eleven. And"—her voice faltered—"there's little prospect of a dowry. We dare not impose upon my aunt more than we have already."

"Perhaps it would be better anyhow to try among the relatives." He raised his wine cup to his lips, stared at it a moment, and then lowered it slowly to the table. "I think you'll find, woman, that after this military appointment of ours, your aunt may express respect, perhaps even pride, that she has had the privilege of having us in her home over the last several years. As for Takiko, she might very well inherit the bulk of your aunt's estate—you know those greedy cousins of yours will want to keep it in the family."

Takiko had heard these dull discussions of marriage too many times to listen again. Her mind was on the music of warfare—a ballad of samurai—the noble Heike crushing the rebellious Genji—her father swinging his great sword, the hero of it all. She shivered with pride. His voice droned on—this cousin was too poor; that one, hopelessly ugly. She became impatient with his going on and on about her stupid marriage when he should be donning his armor and his great horned helmet and riding out to victory, from whence he would return clothed in honor. Then the servants would surely respect her.

She heard the news about the most important event in her short life while eavesdropping. Despite her father's injunction, she was hiding again, this time behind a screen in Lady Uchinaka's music room. She had cleverly concluded that the last place the servants would look for her was in the music room itself. The only problem with the hiding place was that it was almost impossible to leave it unobserved, and she was beginning to get bored, crouched there with nothing to do except to listen to the footsteps of servants shuffling back and forth across the mat floor and down the wooden flooring of the hallway. She wished she had chosen the shed again, where she could have amused herself watching the beetles as they scurried along the rotting timber and disappeared into the cracks in the wall.

Beetles and servants. She put her hand over her mouth to keep from giggling. What did beetles really do once they escaped through the crack out of sight?

"So he's dead?" It was the voice of one of the maids. They had apparently come in to clean the room.

"If his sword and ashes are proof—quite dead." Something turned in Takiko's stomach.

"It's hard to imagine him a hero. I never saw him sober."

"You don't have to be sober to be a hero. Can you fancy a sober officer leading his men straight into the Uji River? The Genji had destroyed the bridge. They say he lost half his force in the crossing."

"But he's a hero?"

"Oh, quite. They killed everyone except the rebel Prince, who killed himself."

"Oh, my!" The two maids finished the task of closing the wooden shutters and lighting a lamp for the room.

Takiko listened to their footsteps in the corridor. There was a cold lump in her stomach which sent a message of ice to her brain: "I wanted him to go. I wanted him to be a hero. I have killed my father." No. She pushed the message away with all the force of her being, jumping out of her hiding place and running down the hallway to her family's rooms.

Several hours later her aunt sent for her. Her mother knelt white-faced in the corner, but this time Lady Uchinaka was kneeling behind the table. Takiko recognized her father's sword beside the small urn.

"Your father has returned in honor." It was all Takiko heard her say, her mind was too busy building a wall between it and the unthinkable messages coming from deep within. She had not killed her father or willed him dead. She had only wanted for him that which he wanted for himself.

He had only asked for two things in life—a son, which neither of his wives had given him, and honor. She could not be the son he wanted, but she could not begrudge him his honor. And she would make a brilliant marriage and give him grandsons and. . . .

Her mother had gotten quickly up and left the room. Takiko half rose to her feet.

"No," said her aunt. "She needs to be alone." The older woman let out a long sigh. "Don't ever love a man, Takiko. They are only grief whether they live or die."

"No, Aunt," she promised solemnly. She must be obedient, her father had said.

"In the end you despise him or yourself." Her aunt sighed again. "There will be no music today." She nodded, dismissing the child from her presence.

In a few days, Takiko came to a new position in the household. At first she rejected the respect of the servants as another of their tricks, but at length she was seduced by it. To be suddenly the daughter of the city's most honored hero — she could not help but relish it after a while. And when the cook persuaded a minstrel to come in and perform for her one of the ballads that were being sung about the city concerning the glorious death of Lord Moriyuki of the Heike clan, she forsook her last nagging doubt. All the servants wept openly when the singer told of the beautiful widow holding her baby son and weeping toward the north, and even Takiko forgave the poet his error, so moved was she to be a part of the drama that caused the city to sob and sing.

But the excitement died down eventually. The servants began to forget how special she was. The cook stopped slipping her sweet bean cakes behind her aunt's back. The gardener was too busy to make toys for her, and the maids' faces lost their expressions of shy respect. And from the north there were rumors of threats. Yoritomo, chief of the Genji, was growing stronger, despite the setback at Uji, and some said he would seek to destroy the family of Moriyuki of the Heike as his first act of vengeance should he enter the capital.

Lady Uchinaka was not a coward, but she was a practical woman. So she allowed a few months to pass after the funeral and then began to talk openly of new living arrangements for the widow and child. Takiko, armed with her father's injunction to take care of her mother, eavesdropped on the two women whenever possible.

"He is not, as I recall, a handsome man, Goro. But he makes an honest living as a potter and stays away from the wine cups. He is not, of course, a samurai, but he is a distant relative of ours, with noble blood. Just recently he wrote asking me to arrange a suitable marriage for him, and since he lives in Shiga some little distance from the city, you and the child would be safe there in case of attack."

There was no reply from her mother.

"He is not handsome, you understand. But in your position. . . ." Even Takiko knew what her mother's position was. A widow of twenty-seven with a daughter of eleven was not considered a prize on the marriage market.

"Then you are willing?"

"Yes." Her mother's reply was barely audible.

"Good. I'll write our cousin at once."

When her mother officially approached her to tell her of her plan to marry again, Takiko, no longer the center of attention in the household, was more than bored with life at her aunt's and eager to be on her way. She could hardly disguise her delight.

"Good. I'm tired of living here with Aunt."

"There will not be so many servants."

"Servants are silly."

"He—he will not be handsome like your father."

"I know."

Her mother gave her a sharp look. "And he is not a samurai."

"Then what is he?"

"A—a potter." The widow stumbled over the word. But the child was already intrigued by the idea. In her life she had chiefly known two kinds of men—noblemen, whose occupation was vague and somehow calculated to make their wives weep; and servants, whose faces and behavior were grave and proper before her aunt, but who had often failed to disguise the contempt they felt for her unfortunate family. She would like to know a man who really did something that she could see, like the gardener who was too busy for her now. Perhaps the potter would let her help him. Perhaps he would even teach her how to make things. She was clever and quick. Her aunt always said so. She'd like making beautiful cups or whatever it was that potters make.

Lady Uchinaka sent off the bride-to-be in her own carriage with three attendants, and she donated some clothing and lacquerware and a few bolts of material, so that the younger woman would not shame her for having nothing in the way of a dowry. All Lady Moriyuki's former possessions had been sold to pay her husband's debts in those dark days before her aunt had reluctantly taken them under her roof.

Takiko was to follow her mother in a few weeks, as her aunt thought it best for her mother to have time to settle herself in her new life before bringing her daughter into it.

The attendants whom Lady Uchinaka sent returned from the country after a two weeks' stay with the bridal couple, and of course the servants gathered in the kitchen for a full report on their trip.

"And what does the bridegroom look like?" asked the cook. "I've heard he's part Korean."

"Part monkey, more than likely," replied one of the attendants. The other two gasped, then let out a shriek of laughter.

No one knew that the child Takiko was listening at the door.

TWO
The Farm

Takiko crept away to the quarters that she had once shared with her mother. Part of her mind tried to reject the conversation she had just overheard. No one had claimed that the potter was handsome. Her mother had prepared her for that. But she was angry at the laughter. The servants were always forgetting their place, the insolent wretches. Her mother was a noblewoman, and her father had been a samurai of the Heike. How dared they despise her mother?

She was glad she was leaving them. Even her aunt, who seemed to dote on her, was now apparently quite eager to push her out of sight now that her father was dead. Takiko hated her. She hated them all. She would be only too glad when her mother sent for her and she could leave this house of hypocrisy. She packed and repacked her tiny trunk. The only thing of value in it was her father's long sword. She took it out tenderly and polished the lacquered sheath with the sleeve of her garment. And when she did so, she feared that her own tears for him had been hypocritical. Hadn't she loved being the daughter of a hero? She began to weep fresh, angry tears and beg his spirit to forgive her.

For the next few days she kept herself aloof from the rest of the household. They thought she missed her mother, so no one made anything of it. And when word came that her mother would like her to come to the country, her delight at the news confirmed this notion that the child was longing for her mother's breast.

Her aunt wept, kissing and patting her until Takiko grew impatient. At last she was put into the ox-drawn carriage, and Choko was sent along as her companion.

"You're not to peep through the curtains. It's not proper," Choko scolded, but Takiko ignored her. For one who had rarely been outside her aunt's gate this trip was an adventure to be relished. She was certainly not going to let the scruples of some silly servant girl keep her from seeing the sights.

As the ox plodded through the city streets, a young boy walking beside to guide its way, the curtains at the rear of the carriage were parted ever so slightly so that a bright dark eye could spy upon a forbidden world.

The ox driver led the beast down the length of Seventh Avenue past the gates of wealthy houses to the long street called Kawaramachi, which bounded the city on the east and ran beside the Kamo River. The driver shouted to clear the way for the carriage, and the delighted Takiko found herself nearly eye to eye with street merchants hawking their wares, painted ladies from the bawdy district on Sixth Avenue, runny-nosed children who caught her stare and returned it with a stare and a giggle of their own.

"They can see you! Close the curtains!" Choko pulled at Takiko's sleeve.

"Leave me alone!" Takiko jerked loose from the servant's grasp. Nothing would make her close the curtains on this marvelous new world of noises and smells.

"Move out of the way," the ox driver shouted, but the crowds on Gojo Bridge could not be hurried. There were soldiers among them, not in battle dress, but well armed. Troubles continued in the north. Yoritomo grew bolder by the month. At last the carriage had made its way to the opposite bank where rose the walls of a huge estate.

"Look, Choko, quick. Is that the palace?"

The annoyed Choko pretended not to hear.

"I'll open the curtains all the way if you don't answer."

Choko crawled to the rear and peeked out. "No, no, the palace is back in the city. This must be Rokuhara."

"Move, Choko. I want to see, too." And both girls peered out, one head above the other, straining to see what they could of the mansion built by Lord Kiyomori, chief of the Heike.

"If he still lived here, Yoritomo would not dare attack the city." Takiko unconsciously quoted her aunt.

"Pooh," Choko replied irreverently. "What could an old man like that do against Yoritomo?"

The fact that the servant was probably both right and disrespectful irritated Takiko, but she did not know how to reply.

They had left the city behind. In the late October sun, persimmons shone like great orange jewels in their trees. The rice had all been harvested, but straw remained, drying on racks in the fields. Here and there farmers could be seen digging turnips or hanging roots to dry for the winter. Smoke from the huts reminded the girls that rice was being cooked, so they dropped the curtain for a time and ate the rice cakes and pickled vegetables that the cook had provided for their lunch. There were two sweet bean cakes for a special treat, and at Takiko's urging the servant girl shared one of these as well.

Choko licked her fingers. "We should be there before long now."

The words landed like a cold lump in Takiko's stomach. A few hours ago she had been eager to be rid of Choko and all of her aunt's household, but suddenly they seemed quite safe and dear. "Choko, could you stay here for a few days? Until I get settled?"

Choko stopped licking and looked at her kindly. "No, Takiko. The ox carriage will be going back tomorrow, and I have to go with it. You'll be all right. Your mother is there."

The child nodded. Choko closed and tied up the lacquer lunchbox. "Someday you'll come and visit us in the city. You'll see." She glanced at the child, but Takiko was staring at her lap. "Perhaps there will be other children for you to play with here. It was lonely for you at Lady Uchinaka's. You'll have a new life. Cheer up, won't you?"

Takiko managed a smile. They heard the driver calling, and the ox carriage came to a halt. "Are we there?" she whispered.

Choko stuck her head out the front curtains. "Yes," she replied. She and the driver consulted for a moment as to the proper etiquette and concluded that Choko should go ahead and announce their arrival and the boy would bring the carriage slowly along after a few minutes' wait. Choko straightened her hair and dress, disarranged by the long bumpy ride. Then she carefully combed out Takiko's long hair and retied her sash. "Everything will be all right, you'll see." She patted the younger girl's knee and then disappeared out the curtains.

Takiko tried to sit quietly in the darkened carriage while she waited, but her stomach churned more now the carriage was still than it had on all the long, bumpy journey. At last she peeped out the front curtains and could see in the distance a tiny village and somewhat to the right of it a thatched-roof farmhouse, but there was no sign of her mother or anyone else. The ox munched contentedly on rice straw, and the driver sat on the roadside leisurely eating his lunch. As he finished, Takiko dropped the curtain and sat properly, waiting for the trip to resume, but nothing happened. When she could stand it no longer, she peeped out again, and there he remained, carefully picking his teeth. She could have screamed. After what seemed an eternity, he spit out the toothpick and strolled back toward the carriage. Takiko jerked the curtain into position just before he gave his call and the carriage lunged forward nearly spilling her backward.

The road into the farmhouse was rutted, and the carriage bumped, so that all Choko's efforts to make her presentable came to nothing. A wheel dropped into one great hole with such force that Takiko bounced up, hitting her head on the top of the carriage. She did what she could to smooth her hair, but she was near tears from the pain.

The driver called the halt. She waited, her heart pounding now as well as her head. Someone pulled the back curtain.

"Welcome, little mistress." A kind peasant face bent into the opening. "I am called Fusa. Here, give me your hand, and I'll help you down."

"Where is my mother?" asked the child, not moving.

"Waiting impatiently for you." And with that the large woman scooped her up and deposited her on the ground.

The only other person in sight besides the ox driver was Choko, standing shyly by the front door, though out of the corner of her eye Takiko thought she saw a little brown creature scurrying around to the back of the farm-house.

Despite her protests, the woman called Fusa undressed her and scrubbed her and plunged her into a steaming wooden tub before she would take her to see her mother.

"Why, she'd never recognize you under all this dust!"

But at last, red and tingling from her bath, and dressed in a clean garment, she was led by Fusa to her mother's chamber, where the two of them threw their arms around each other's necks and wept without shame.

"So this is Takiko."

Takiko turned and saw through her tears what she had only glimpsed earlier. He stood hardly taller than herself, but his chest and head were as large as those of a well-built man. His arms, powerfully muscled, hung down nearly to his knees, and his eyes were slits in a broad face that was brown as a chestnut. He came in and knelt beside her.

"This is my husband, Taki Chan," her mother said quietly as though this were a simple fact.

The creature made a face with its narrow eyes and large mouth which it seemed to intend as a smile. "What a pretty child." It raised one giant hand as though to stroke her hair, but Takiko, horrified lest it touch her, shrank against her mother.

"No," she whispered. "Don't let it touch me."

The hand dropped immediately.

"Speak to your father, Takiko." She had never heard her gentle mother speak so sternly. She was doomed in hell, and her mother belonged to the devils.

"No," she shrieked, "no!" and clung to her mother.

"Forgive her, my lord, she is tired."

"Yes. So am I." Goro the potter rose abruptly and stumped from the room.

THREE
A New Year

"You must stop crying now, Takiko." Chieko pushed her daughter gently away and rose to her feet. "I will ask Fusa to bring you some tea, and then she will lay out your bed. You seem very tired."

Takiko sniffled and wiped her face. "No, I'm not tired."

"I must believe you are tired, Takiko. Otherwise your rudeness would be unforgivable."

She could hardly bear the coldness in her mother's tone. "No, Mother, don't leave me." She reached for the hem of her mother's robe.

Chieko knelt beside her, taking her outstretched hand. "Please, Taki Chan," she whispered, "for my sake, try to like him. He will be a good father to you if you let him."

"My father is a samurai!"

"If you are the daughter of a samurai, then you know how a sword must be judged." She got up again. "Fusa will see to your needs until you are ready to join your father and me." Then more gently, "I hope that will be soon, Taki Chan. I've missed you." And she was gone.

Something had happened to her mother in these weeks. Perhaps the potter was a devil and had bewitched her. Her soft, weeping mother had disappeared, and someone strong and cold had taken over her mother's beautiful body. The explanation satisfied Takiko's raging, but in the cool places of her mind, she knew it was false. Her mother had only been hard toward her after she had screamed at the . . . , at the . . . , the potter. Everything in her rejected the word *father*, for she was unable to consider that the monster was indeed her mother's husband and her own stepfather.

The cheerful Fusa brought rice tea and sweet bean cakes and set them on the table. She left the room and returned with a lamp.

"You must eat, little one. You are far too thin." But Takiko sat sullenly before the small table with her lips pinched tightly together. The woman bustled about the room, closing the blinds as the sun was already setting. "Would you like a brazier? These autumn evenings get chilly, don't they?"

Takiko shook her head.

"What did you say?"

"I'm not cold."

The woman came over and knelt beside her. "You're not hungry?"

"No."

"It's hard for you, isn't it, little one?" Takiko wanted to weep at these kind words, but she took protection behind her anger. She would not be seduced by kindness. This woman was part of the terrible household here. She maintained her stony silence.

The woman sighed. "As you will," she shrugged. "Your bed is laid out in the east room. Will you sleep now, little mistress?"

Takiko got up without a word and followed the servant through the long wooden corridor. So resigned was she to despair and loneliness that at the sight awaiting her in the small room they entered, she gave a little cry of surprise. For there was dear, familiar Choko kneeling before a low table covered with food. Her chopsticks were poised halfway to her mouth, which was obviously stuffed.

"Takiko." Her mouth was too full to speak further, so she hastily swallowed. "I thought you would eat with the mistress."

"The young mistress was not hungry," said Fusa.

Choko's eyebrows went up. And Takiko, looking at the rice and fish with the smell of the hot soup invading her nostrils, thought she might die of hunger and frustration.

"Could you eat a little?" Fusa asked gently. "So Choko won't feel embarrassed?"

"Perhaps," she said tightly, "on account of Choko."

"Of course," said Fusa and disappeared.

"What's the matter, Taki Chan? You seem so angry."

"Do I?"

"Is your mother well?"

"I suppose so."

"And her husband?"

At this question Takiko lifted her eyes from her lap. "Have you seen him, Choko?"

"No."

Takiko looked carefully around and then leaned over the table. "He—he's monstrous," she whispered.

"What do you mean, monstrous?"

"*Shhh.*" She was terrified lest Fusa return and overhear her. "He's about my height, but his head and shoulders are huge and his arms hang down like a—like a monkey's."

"That one is the master?"

"You saw him then?"

"I got a glimpse of him, but I never supposed. . . ."

"He frightened me, and now my mother is angry with me, not him." She would have begun to cry, but the voice of Fusa stopped her.

"Excuse me."

"Yes, bring it in. Thank you." Choko spoke in perfect imitation of Lady Uchinaka, a tone that prompted the country woman to serve the food and leave quickly.

"What will I do, Choko? I can't stay here."

"Eat your supper, Takiko. You'll feel better."

The child was hungry despite everything and so began to eat, but she kept her eyes on Choko's face. Choko tried to look thoughtful, as though pondering some solution, but she knew of none. She had been sent to deliver the child to her mother. This she had done. She was powerless to interfere. So though in her manner and words she sought to comfort the child, she knew there was no escape for Takiko.

For herself there was escape, and she chose to take it, slipping out of the room before dawn, so that when Takiko awoke and called for her, she and the ox carriage had already two hours' start on their journey home.

When Takiko was informed that Choko and the carriage had left long before, the rage of the night before settled like a cold rock in her chest. She obeyed Fusa's every suggestion in an attitude of quiet despair. Thus her soft city garments were exchanged for trousers and blouse of homespun. Her long hair was tied back from her face with a scarlet cord, and after a bowl of hot bean soup, she followed Fusa to the kitchen.

"We all work here, even the mistress."

"I understand."

"Good. I don't suppose you know how to do anything yet."

"I can play the koto."

The woman laughed good-naturedly. "We'll save that for New Year's. Here, I'll begin by showing you how to shell these beans."

Takiko was agile-fingered which delighted the woman. And the morning quickly passed.

"I think you have forgotten to be unhappy," the woman said to her over their noonday rice.

Takiko was startled to realize it was true. It was hard to think of this busy, cheerful woman as one of her enemies. But when Fusa went on to suggest that she might take supper with her mother and stepfather, she stiffened.

"In the city, my father did not eat with women."

"In the city, life is very formal. When your mother came, there were only the two of them. The master felt it would be lonely for her to eat by herself. Now they are in the habit. You are to be permitted to join them, for you will soon be a young woman, you know."

"I'd rather eat with you, Fusa."

"As you will."

The days went by, and Takiko saw her mother from time to time, but it was only briefly and in passing. Her mother kept busy, mostly with sewing and mending chores neglected since the death of her new husband's mother the year before. Fusa was too busy in the kitchen and on the farm to see to these. Takiko followed the older woman about and learned quite quickly to do the tasks she assigned her.

Once as the two of them knelt over a sickly baby pig, they were aware of a shadow standing over them.

Takiko looked up into the nut-brown face. She cringed despite herself. The narrow eyes tightened into a slit.

"She is a good help to me, master."

"Good," he said sharply, stumping away. "Good."

But for the most part, Takiko lived her life quite apart from Chieko and her husband. Goro took his turn in the field along with his serfs, and most of the rest of the time he spent in the hut that housed his craft. The kiln was built into the side of a hill by the turnip patch, and the little man could be seen bearing a tray of pottery to the site, overseeing the firing, and then several days later carefully removing the fired pieces from the cooled kiln. Fusa explained proudly that the master had sent to Korea for a craftsman to build the kiln for him, and the wheel upon which he made the earthenware had come all the way from China. The old master had given it to Goro when he was still a boy. "And now," Fusa boasted, "my master can make anything he chooses."

It was not an empty claim, for unlike Lady Uchinaka's household, which used wooden and lacquer utensils, the household of Goro used vessels and jugs, cups and bowls of black-glazed earthenware, all from the potter's own wheel. Some pieces were sold to neighbors, and a few were deemed worthy by their creator to seek a sale in the capital.

But Goro never took them there himself. The merchant Kamaji, a friend of his father's before the old master's death, came twice a year to take back to his shop in Heiankyō the wares Goro chose to send there.

Handling the pottery everyday as she did, Takiko remembered her childish ambition to see it made, perhaps even to make some herself. But, of course, everything had turned out so differently from those daydreams at Lady Uchinaka's. There was no possibility now that she would ever see it made—nor would she want to.

Sometimes during that first winter when the cold was so intense that she would cry from it, she would recall other winters when she had shared her mother's bed. And she would long for the warmth of her mother's body and almost repent the anger she felt against her. But she did not dare to go to her mother in the middle of the night, and by morning the feeling would have eased and the busyness of the day would be its own comfort.

New Year's preparations began early, for there was much to do and fewer hands to do it than in the city. Takiko helped Fusa sweep and scrub the house, room by room. Quilts were taken apart. The stuffing was aired, and the covers were carefully washed. Then stuffing and covers were turned over to Chieko for restitching. After the bedding, every quilted garment in the house was taken apart, washed, stretched to dry, and then resewn.

Two weeks before the holiday, Fusa began preparing the food. The usual fare in the country was rather plain compared to the food at Lady Uchinaka's. But during New Year's no pains were spared, especially this New Year's, for Goro viewed it as a protracted wedding feast and ordered that enough food be provided so that every peasant in the district could join the merriment at the farmhouse.

Fusa's married daughter and two granddaughters
came to help in the kitchen. The children worked hard,
but if Takiko spoke to them, they dissolved into nervous
giggles, so she soon gave up trying to be friendly. She
was too busy to be bothered with such silliness.

When the time came to pound the New Year's rice
cakes, two of Fusa's nephews appeared with heavy
wooden mallets. Fusa put steamed rice into a huge
wooden bowl, and the two lads began beating it, singing
a toneless chant as they rhythmically pounded it into a
glutenous mass. The cooking and pounding went on for
two days, for Fusa was determined not to embarrass the
master by running out of rice cakes for his guests.

Takiko meanwhile was put to work making decora-
tions for the door. Fusa had to direct, to be sure, for she
had never been entrusted with such a task before. As
Fusa boasted, Takiko's fingers were as quick as her mind,
and the rope she fashioned to guard the house from evil
was praised by all. Even the two granddaughters stopped
giggling long enough to finger the arrangement of straw
tufts and paper prayers and to breathe a sigh of admiration.

Takiko blushed with pleasure, then to cover her shyness asked Fusa what her next task should be.

"I have brought the old mistress's koto from the storehouse. No one has played it since her death."

"I'm out of practice, Fusa. I would be ashamed to
play it."

"It would give the master such pleasure."

Takiko hesitated.

"And your mother."

The child's eyes remained on her hands which she
twisted in front of her body.

"And me."

She looked up smiling. "For your sake, Fusa. But I'm afraid I'll only embarrass you."

"Never."

At midnight the distant temple bell rang out the one hundred and eight strokes that hailed a New Year. Lying between her quilts, Takiko listened. The New Year had begun. She must make a new start. It would please Fusa. And her mother. As she was falling back to sleep, she had the feeling that her mother's arms were about her once again.

At daybreak Fusa's nephews raced to the willow spring to bring the freshest, sweetest water for the feast. And when Takiko entered the great room, carrying a tray of soup, she found it crowded with peasants, presided over by a beaming Goro.

She put down her tray, and kneeling before him, bowed her head to the floor. Then with a great push of her will, she said the traditional greeting. "A New Year has dawned. This year, again, I beg your kindness."

The potter returned the bow and the greeting.

Takiko did not lift her head, but remained head to floor, and then whispered, "And for my rudeness of the past year, I beg my father's forgiveness."

There was a silence between them which the noisy chattering crowd did not obscure. At last she heard him clear his throat and then the murmur, "There is nothing to forgive, my child."

She got up and ran to the kitchen as fast as she could.

"They want you to play for them, little mistress." Fusa came to where Takiko was boiling dried fish to make more lucky soup for the unending stream of guests.

"Now?" Takiko looked up, wiping perspiration from her face on her apron. Fusa was smiling broadly. She knows, thought the girl. "The mistress asked especially that you come. Here"—the woman began to untie the apron—"you've worked long enough. I'll have my nephew fetch the koto from your room."

Takiko entered the room shyly and knelt close to the door, but her mother had been watching for her and got up at once and came to greet her. "A New Year has dawned," she began, but instead of finishing, she put her arms around Takiko and hid her tears in her child's shoulder.

"Come," she said quickly, ashamed to have displayed her feeling before the celebrating peasants. "You must come up here with us." She led Takiko to the table where Goro sat. He was in great spirits; the wine had turned his brown face a dark red.

"First eat and then play," he commanded, his hand sweeping out toward the koto which Fusa's nephew had brought.

Takiko tried to smile and protest politely while the little man piled her plate higher and higher. "Just a little soup," she said.

"Nonsense. This is a celebration."

And despite her protests, she found she could eat and even take a taste of the wine, which was warm and sweet and turned her shyness into something like contentment.

So that by the time she was asked to play, she did so without self-consciousness and so lost herself in the rippling chords that she began to sing, softly at first and then quite naturally. She did not play the Chinese classics so loved by Lady Uchinaka, but a song she had learned in her aunt's kitchens. It was a ballad of a samurai who returns from a glorious victory only to find that his beloved is dying.

As full of wine and high spirits as they were, the crowd listened quite humbly, and when it was over, there was a lot of noisy nose blowing and respectful swearing. The peasants had never heard anything like it, they said. It was music fit for the Emperor himself, a feast of beauty.

She played everything she knew, and when that was not enough, she began again and played it all over. Their admiration warmed her more than the wine. When they asked for still more, she probably would have gone on and on, but her mother protested: "She's hardly had time to eat. Please, let her rest." And so with a twinge of disappointment she left the instrument and came back to Goro's table.

"You have given us great pleasure," he said as she knelt before him.

"You are too kind," she said, dropping her eyes.

Her mother reached over and touched her arm lightly. "It will be a good year," she said.

Takiko, feeling the caress of her hand and voice, was completely content. The foolish estrangement of the past months seemed to drop away. Even as she stole a glance at Goro, she wondered how he could ever have frightened her. He was monstrous, shriveled, and ugly, but surely not terrifying. She had been a stupid child, but that was all in the past. He no longer frightened her. For her mother's sake she would call him father and treat him with respect, even eat with him if her mother wished. She lost herself in happy daydreams of her mother's teaching her to sew and weave. She would ask the potter if she could watch him work. It might please him. It would certainly make her mother happy.

". . . a toast to the New Year," Goro was saying in a loud voice to quiet the crowd into attention. "In February, plum blossoms; in April, cherry blossoms; and in August, a son!"

A cry of congratulation went up. For a moment Takiko was stunned, not comprehending; then she saw her mother's face, modestly bowed but with such a look of pride on it that there was no mistaking the meaning — a look that tore the fabric of Takiko's daydreams, leaving her stripped and cheated.

FOUR
Ichiro

By the time of the early summer rains, Chieko was so swollen with child that Takiko was embarrassed to look at her directly. Fusa made no secret of the fact that she believed it to be a huge and healthy boy, and her own joy at the prospect would not be dimmed by the child's quiet. So Takiko often left the cheerful chatter of the kitchen and retreated to her own room, damp and gloomy as the continuous rains made it seem. To comfort herself a little, she would practice on the koto, though not the formal Chinese music that Lady Uchinaka had so painstakingly taught her, pushing her small fingers down upon the strings until they hurt. No, more and more she found herself playing songs she had heard in the kitchens at Lady Uchinaka's or the country music that Fusa sang as she worked. Sometimes she would simply let her fingers trail over the strings, until they spun a melody all their own and somehow her spirit would be drawn into the vibrating chords and she would lose all sense of time and space outside the shimmering cocoon of the music. Here there was no pain, except the exquisite pain of the songs themselves, and to this she freely poured herself out.

"You spend too much time with your music," her mother chided gently at supper one night. Takiko looked up quickly, surprised and grateful that her mother had noticed.

"But such music it is." Goro spoke so softly that she wondered later if she had really heard him say it.

By July the rains were long forgotten in the exuberance with which the household—all but Takiko—awaited the baby's birth. From some dark closet Goro had hauled bolts of beautiful silk and finespun cotton, and from this treasure Chieko had fashioned enough tiny garments to clothe all the children in the Imperial pavilion. Goro had made on his wheel a perfect little bowl and cup and plate, each with his characteristic brilliant black glaze, but done in miniature.

Fusa, though she denied any skill in needlework, quilted bedding and cleaned the house as though it were New Year's. Takiko helped as always, and no one seemed to notice the heaviness in her.

"Takiko." She woke with a start at the sound of Goro's voice outside her door.

"Yes, Father?"

"It has begun."

"Oh?" It took her a minute to focus on what he was saying. "My mother, is my mother all right?" She sat up straight in her covers.

"Fusa says everything is fine. We can only wait."
There was a silence. Takiko sat puzzling for a moment
before she understood. "Would you like me to wait with
you?" she asked.

"It would comfort me," he said quietly.

She dressed quickly, a flutter of excitement in her
stomach. When she opened the door, Goro entered with a
lamp. In the shadowy light he looked uglier than usual.
There were lines of fatigue in his broad face, and his tiny
eyes seemed dull.

"The child is large," he said. "It may take many
hours."

Takiko got tea for him, and opened the shutters. In
silence they watched the first red light of morning stain
the sky. How much longer? she wondered. She had not
wanted the baby to come at all, but now she resented its
delay.

Goro gave a low groan.

"What is it?"

His head was buried in his massive hands, and his
great shoulders were shaking.

"Father, what is it?"

"Suppose, oh, suppose, Takiko that it is"—he
lifted his head and looked into her eyes as she knelt
before him—"if it is like me, I shall want to . . . to kill
it."

"No!" she breathed.

He reached over and touched her knee. "You are so
beautiful. How can you know?" He removed his hand
with a little shudder. "But, of course, I would never harm
it. If your mother can bear with me—" He shook himself.
"You must forgive me, I am very tired. Would you play
for me?"

He stretched out on the floor as she began to play

softly. Then before long, she lost herself in the music and forgot him, striking the strings with power, her voice weaving in and out of the pattern of rippling sound. When she remembered him again, he was asleep, so she covered him with her quilt, tiptoed to the kitchen, and began to prepare breakfast. Someone would surely want to eat eventually, and she at least was already quite hungry.

"It's a boy! A beautiful, huge, healthy boy!" Fusa burst into the kitchen.

"The Gods are good." Takiko said it quite sincerely, with the vision of the haunted Goro clearly in her mind. It was only much later that she remembered her own handsome father whose chief ambition had been to hear such news and who had died without an heir. That Goro should so swiftly be given what had always been denied her own father seemed so unfair that she had to fight a kind of bitterness whenever she looked at Goro's beautiful son.

Despite the size of the infant, which everyone marveled over, Chieko recovered her strength quickly. She would not be persuaded to get a wet nurse, but took on the task of satisfying from her own breasts the little giant's tremendous appetite. It was a task that took almost all her time and energy, so that Goro had the leisure that fall to teach Takiko not only Japanese script but nearly a thousand Chinese characters as well.

Takiko was thus the only female she had ever known who could write Chinese characters. She took enormous pride in the fact, and badgered the little man every day to teach her more, so that she could read the dusty scrolls in the storehouse as well as begin to write imitations of love poems that Goro had taught her.

The potter liked her company, and even invited her into his shop to watch him work. Once inside the door,

Takiko gave herself up to a mysterious new world. Goro sat cross-legged on a tiny platform. Before him was the wheel. This was like a large plate set upon a spindle. Upon the center of the wheel he slapped a ball of clay. Around the edge were four holes. Into one of these, he would insert a short stick and send the wheel spinning so fast that it could hardly be seen. Then, as if by a magic spell, something would begin to take form under the potter's huge hands. Sometimes he would shout, "What will it be?" And she would cry, "A jug!" or "A cup!" or "A bowl!" And to her never-ending delight, whatever she ordered would rise up out of the spinning clay.

Bit by bit, he began to teach her how. Crouched behind her, he would insert the stick and set the wheel to spinning. Then his huge hands over her small ones, he helped her bring the clay up, thumbs down to make a hole, a slight pressure to change the shape or make the lip on a jug. She had the same feeling of power that her music gave her. She was inside the clay, yet master and creator of it.

"Watch out!"

But it was too late. Lost in fancy, she had drawn a jug to an impossible height, and the thin clay wall collapsed in ruin on the still-spinning wheel.

"Don't laugh at me," she pouted.

"I'm not laughing," he protested, but his stomach was shaking and his small eyes dancing. "Here, try again." He carefully scraped the evidence of her failure off the wheel and slapped fresh clay in its place. Later he would patiently reverse creation, turning her fallen jug back to its primordial mass out of which some new miracle might spring up from his wheel. Nothing was ever wasted.

Sometimes at his urging she tried again, but often

she pretended to be angry at his laughter, and flounced off, really angry with herself that she who did everything else so quickly, should meet defeat over a clay pot.

In a few days' time, Goro would tease her into coming back, and over the months she began to make sturdy vessels. No one who knew would have confused her work with the potter's, although they all wore the same brilliant black glaze. There was an artistry in his shapes that even her unpracticed eye was forced to acknowledge. But nonetheless, she was making cups and jugs that survived all the rigors of firing and even came to be used around the farmhouse.

Goro praised her extravagantly. But it annoyed her that he did so. It really confirmed her fears that the pottery was less than good, for he never praised her music in this way, and she knew in her heart that he truly admired it.

Life passed quietly in Goro's household. There was a famine that year in many of the provinces. And men came from as far away as the capital to buy grain and vegetables from his lands. For along with all the other miracles the Gods performed for the little potter, they gave him a bountiful crop and kept the curse of plague from his door. Fusa said it was because the Gods looked down and saw this one man of peace in a nation gone mad with war. At any rate, famine forced an armistice that neither Emperor nor general could declare.

Meantime the child Ichiro grew into a beautiful, completely spoiled first son. He talked and walked early, with Chieko and Fusa clucking over every word and every step.

Takiko's own body was changing, and with it came more confusion of feeling. Sometimes she would watch her mother nursing the noisy, greedy little king, and something like tenderness would stir in her own young breasts. But at other times the boy's imperious demands and the women's devotion to them would annoy her, and she would seek out Goro, telling herself that he treated her more like a son than he did this brat of a man-child who was his own.

She was partially right. Goro was shy with the boy. He had had no brothers and sisters and had never been around babies or even young children. He left the care of his son entirely to the women, not even daring to pick him up.

Then one day when Goro and Takiko were working in the shop, Fusa burst in. "Ichiro! Ichiro! We can't find him!"

Takiko and Goro jumped up and raced into the courtyard where a distracted Chieko was scurrying about, peering behind sacks and into barrels.

"He was here." Chieko said. "Not a moment ago."

Without a word Goro began to run. Above his short legs, his large torso swung crazily. Takiko watched for a moment and then took off after him. Across the rice-field path he went with Takiko just behind. He was headed for the river. Takiko dared not think what he had found when she saw his body slide down over the bank out of sight.

She reached the top of the bank and stood there panting. Below, Goro held a startled Ichiro, who was kicking and struggling to get free of his iron grip.

"You fool!" The little man was shouting. "You silly little fool! You might have fallen in and drowned."

"No! No!" The boy cried, beating his father's shoulder with his fists.

With one large hand, the potter grasped Ichiro's arm.

Then he reached up and pulled a switch from the willow tree above his head.

Takiko gasped, but Goro never looked up. In a quiet fury he stung the child's fat little legs until red marks stood out against the tan flesh.

At last he dropped the switch and swung the screaming child to his huge shoulder. "Tell them my son is safe," he said, looking up at Takiko. There were tears rolling down his brown cheeks.

The girl nodded. Something in her throat stopped any words that might have come. She fled back to the farmhouse with the father and son following slowly behind. From that day it was Ichiro who followed the potter wherever he went. And Takiko began to learn how to sew and weave.

FIVE
To the Capital

She was thirteen the autumn that the merchant Kamaji came to buy pottery from Goro. He had been there each spring and autumn, but this was the first time that he truly saw Takiko. Before that, she had been a child, in manner as much boy as girl, but suddenly the merchant saw a beautiful young woman with a flawless porcelain face and large shining eyes. The long hair was brushed to a brilliant black gloss and fell gently over her breasts as she leaned over the koto. And the music which came from the slight body and the long instrument was enough to remind him of Benten, the daughter of the Dragon King, Goddess of Music and giver of wealth and romance.

And since the merchant had drunk freely of Goro's

best wines, his tongue was loosed and his praise extravagant. "You must find her a place in the court," he said. "Such beauty, such talent, are of the Gods."

Goro and Chieko looked at each other with troubled faces, but the merchant went on to promise that he himself would find a worthy setting for this jewel of heaven.

Takiko could not be blamed for being flattered. She had been in the country now for more than two years and far from the easy words of the city. It was a little frightening, but still, if she had such beauty and such talent, wasn't it right that she should share it? Her boredom with sewing and weaving, her suppressed jealousy of the position Ichiro had seized in his father's heart—these played a part to be sure, but mostly her eager acceptance of the merchant's words was born from her new womanhood and her need to have it acknowledged and praised. Fusa and Goro liked her because she was clever and eager. Her mother liked her because mothers must. But who liked her because her hair shone and her breasts made a gentle sloping line under her garments? Indeed, who would ever notice here? Fusa's clottish nephews?

The merchant, who had high-born connections, made arrangements for Takiko to go to the house of Prince Kira, a younger brother of Go Shirakawa, the Retired Emperor. There she would serve as a lady-in-waiting to Princess Aoi, his wife. At Chieko's insistence no mention would be made of the girl's real father; she was to be presented as a relative of Goro's, of noble blood but limited means. Since Goro's family was neither Heike nor Genji, the girl would not be thought to belong to either clan and would remain safe no matter which side won the power struggle that was beginning again in earnest. If the struggle turned into war, no one would be safe, yet neither Chieko nor Goro could face this possibility. They were reluctant to let her go because they would miss her, but in the light of the opportunity that the merchant had arranged, their reluctance seemed selfish. And then the girl herself was so eager to return to the capital. So, although Chieko wept and Goro argued, in the end they let her go. In the ox cart returning to Heiankyō, Takiko never once peeked out the curtains.

Princess Aoi was a tall woman. She was much praised for her hair, which hung thick and black well past her knees. She had a carefully powdered face and painted eyebrows and lips, and in the fashion of high-born married women, her front teeth were blackened.

The serving girl who brought Takiko into the Princess's chamber left quickly, and after the formal greeting, Princess Aoi and Takiko sat back upon their knees, their faces composed, their minds busily sizing each other up.

Underneath her best garments, Takiko's heart was wildly pounding. The Princess seemed as beautiful as a snow-capped mountain peak, and just as cold and remote. She had long white fingers, which were now curled about a silk fan, and as she slowly fanned, the twelve layers of silk garments showed at her sleeve and made Takiko feel shame at her own garments, which until that moment she had regarded as quite pretty.

"I see they have bathed you," the elegant woman said at last.

"Yes, your Highness," Takiko whispered, afraid now that her speech would appear rough and uncultured.

"They should have provided you with fresh garments. Yours must be dusty."

Dusty? Takiko was mortified. The clothes she had worn on the journey had been given a servant for washing. Those she now wore, she had taken fresh from her trunk so as to impress her new mistress. Did she appear so unacceptable then? She was seized with a great desire to get up and run—all the way back to Goro's farm if necessary. In her mind she could see herself racing across Gojo Bridge, past Rokuhara Mansion, through the dirt roads of the countryside beside the river, then across the rice paths beyond the village to the thatched farmhouse. How glad they all would be to see her! Even little Ichiro would grasp her knees and cry, "Sister! Sister!" She would never resent him again. He was only a baby after all. And Goro would be so glad to see her back that he would insist that they begin their Chinese lessons again. They would make pottery together—such magnificent pottery that all over the land they would become famous for it. Fusa would hug her and pet her, and her mother would weep with joy. Her mother. . . .

"Isn't that so?" From underneath the perfectly painted eyebrows, the sharp eyes looked down. The Princess was waiting for a reply.

Takiko's mouth went dry. "I beg your Highness's pardon." She bowed her head and tried to clear her throat without making a vulgar noise.

"I said"—the voice went through the girl's body like a winter wind—"I said that we would have to get rid of those garments and find something more suitable for your new estate."

"As you say, your Highness." But as she said the words, she was seized with a sudden yearning to wear her own clothes, dear familiar garments, lovingly made by her mother's own hands. Later she wished that she had had the courage to speak out—to ask the Princess to let her keep them. The Princess herself was a mother—surely she would have honored a daughter's sentimental wish—but Takiko had been too terrified to ask, so that when she awoke the next morning, her clothes were gone, and in their place lay twelve exquisite silk garments, which a maid helped her put on in proper order, so that when her sleeve moved a rainbow of silk rippled into view.

The maid began to brush Takiko's hair, handing her a metal mirror so that she could supervise this important task, but the girl, who had not seen a mirror since she left Lady Uchinaka's house, was startled at the face that met hers. *I have become a woman, as beautiful as my mother.* It gave her a little courage, so that when the servant girl asked if this or that was acceptable, she answered with quiet dignity, no longer the mortified child of the day before.

"You are quite beautiful, madam," the maid said.

Takiko smiled at her. "What is your name?"

"Mieko, madam." The girl bowed her head shyly.

"And will you be with me?"

"As your ladyship wishes," replied the girl.

"It would please me very much. I will speak to her Highness."

"Thank you, madam. The Princess will be waiting for you now."

Takiko suppressed a rise of panic. "You must help me, Mieko. What does the Princess expect of me?"

The girl looked up quickly, cocking her head a moment in puzzlement.

"I mean it, Mieko. I have lived in the country where life is much more simple. But I want to please my mistress."

The girl smiled behind her hand. "Madam, you are to do for her what I do for you."

"Then you will teach me?"

Mieko smiled again. "Yes, my lady." She got up. "I will take you there now. There will be other servants, but you are to comb her hair. She is very particular about her hair." The girl looked worried. "Have you ever . . . ?"

"Oh, yes. Every day," replied Takiko. "My own."

"You are looking rested." The Princess was standing in the center of her room while three women dressed her, layer upon layer.

Takiko bowed her head to the mat floor. "Thank you." Her heartbeat quickened, but with Mieko just behind her, the panic of the night before was kept at bay. She remained sitting on her knees while the women finished dressing the Princess. At last the sash was tied, and the Princess knelt before a small, lacquered dressing table.

Takiko felt a gentle prod from behind and realized that Mieko was signaling her. She went to her mistress. "Shall I comb your hair, your Highness?"

Aoi looked down the length of her lovely nose. "Are you quite sure you know how?"

"Let me try, today, madam, and then if you are dissatisfied, I beg you to let me be instructed further."

The Princess gave a sniff and a nod, and picked up her jeweled mirror. Gently Takiko took a small strand of hair and began to comb. Never before on a living person had she seen hair of such length and thickness. There were scrolls depicting such women, but until now she had never seen one in the flesh. She handled her task as Goro handled a delicate vessel on his wheel, forgetting time, forgetting indeed the person under the hair, so absorbed was she in bringing every strand to perfection.

When at last she finished, it was almost with reluctance that she sat back on her heels and let the Princess judge her work in the mirror.

"You have beautiful hair, your Highness," she said.

"So I am often told." But the tone was not quite as cold as the words.

That afternoon a caller was announced for the Princess. Aoi took Takiko with her to the great hall of the women's pavilion. She motioned to the girl to kneel beside her behind the opaque screen designed to hide noble women from the eyes of ever curious male visitors. Once they were set in their places, a man was ushered into the room. Takiko could see his shadowy form kneel and bow before the screen. Then he settled himself back upon his legs and said, "I bring a message to you, madam, from a dear friend."

"Why hasn't your friend written?" Aoi asked.

"You must believe me, madam. He dares not at this time. The political situation is delicate. . . ."

"The political situation is always delicate. Tell your master either to write or to come himself. I find messengers tedious."

"But, madam. . . ."

They could hear him speaking on, arguing for his master, but Aoi had nodded for Takiko to rise silently, and they left him sitting there, talking to empty air.

"I think I would like for you to play for me," the Princess said as they came again to her chambers. "Have your instrument brought into my room." Takiko started to obey. "Wait. First open the doors and the shutters. I find the air suffocating."

Takiko unlatched the paper sliding doors and the wooden shutters behind them that opened onto the central garden. Ice hung from the branches of the weeping cherry tree outside the door. It sparkled in the pale winter sunshine.

"The ice will break the cherry boughs." The Princess's voice was full of melancholy.

"New shoots will appear in the spring," Takiko said, hoping to brighten her mood.

"For the young there is always another spring." The Princess stared out into the garden.

Takiko sent Mieko for her koto. She played to the Princess's unmoving back. At first she played and sang softly only children's songs, hoping to cheer her mistress, but soon the sound of the strings caught her in their spell, and she was taken beyond that room and that place into the birth of heroes and the death of love. The strings wept and cajoled, cried with joy, and laughed with bitterness as Takiko played on, unaware of the crowd of servants gathered in the corridor or of the tears streaking the carefully applied powder on the Princess's face.

She stopped abruptly, suddenly aware that she had played for a long time and the room had turned icy with the shutters thrown open. The strings were still vibrating, so she smothered their trembling with her hands and sat quietly with her head bowed over the instrument.

"Kamaji did not lie." Aoi spoke with her back still turned toward the room. "You play well."

"You flatter me, madam."

"You must play for the Prince. He is fond of music." There was a long silence; the girl waited not knowing what to do. "You may leave," the tall woman said at last.

"Shall I send someone in to close the shutters?"

"No."

"Then if madam will excuse me—" Takiko picked up the koto and carried it awkwardly to her own quarters.

SIX
The Concert

In the household of Prince Kira hardly anyone realized that the famines were over and that the nation was again at war. The Prince himself had recently brought a new consort into the house and was quite taken up with honeymooning. Nearly a generation had passed since Heiankyō itself had witnessed full-scale battles between Genji and Heike, and even those retainers in the city who regarded themselves as warriors were soft-skinned and flabby with no knowledge of defense, much less of combat.

Hostilities were erupting in various parts of the country, but the capital itself was untouched, so that the aristocrats tended to regard the struggle like a sporting event. People took sides but only in order to bet on the outcome. There was never any expectation in those early days that anyone might become personally caught up in the events or that a preference for one side or the other should be taken seriously.

Rumors were passed about as cheerily as one might pass tea cakes. That Yoritomo had built up a great army in the east, that his youngest brother, Yoshitsune, sneaked in and out of the city like a weasel into a chicken house, that the whole city crawled with spies and possible traitors to the Heike cause—these tidbits were consumed with delight, and the man or woman who produced the choicest item of the day was toasted over the wine cups. How exciting it all seemed! And how remote.

To all but Takiko. A vision of her own father seared her mind when she heard the ladies of the court tittering about disemboweled warriors in the north. Kiyomori, the grizzled bear of the Heike, was two years dead, and his son and successor Munemori had sat too long on silken cushions. How could he be a match for the Genji, hardened by years in exile in mountain and wilderness? Yet the proud Munemori had set forth from the capital to engage the large Genji force led by Yoshinaka, the ambitious cousin of Yoritomo, the Genji chief. Only Takiko seemed to tremble for the outcome of these battles.

As late as the week before news of Munemori's defeat reached the capital, life in Prince Kira's household went on its usual dreamy way with no hint of the nightmares to come.

The Prince had prepared a late spring moon-gazing party in honor of his new consort, and Takiko was summoned to play and sing for the royal guests, one of whom was Go Shirakawa, the Retired Emperor and grandfather of the present Emperor, the child Antoku.

Two of the Prince's men were sent to fetch her. They carried the koto, and she followed them to the Prince's quarters, wishing at each step that faithful Mieko was at her heels. The wooden shutters were all open, even though it was night, and from the garden the full moon provided the only light for the gathered guests.

"Ah, little Takiko." She presumed the voice to be that of her master, though she had not met him before. She bowed her head to the mat floor.

"No, look up. I must see this famous face," he said imperiously, the words coming out in puffs on the chill night air.

She looked up, a little frightened by his manner and the imagined stares of the guests in the shadowy light.

"Come closer, over here." He beckoned her toward him. In the moonlight she saw his face, once handsome, now fleshy with large pouting lips. Beside him sat a beautiful young woman, his newest consort. Takiko was startled to realize that despite her painted eyebrows and blackened teeth she was probably not much older than herself.

"Ah, Ukeko," the Prince said. "You are scarcely more than a bride, and already there is a rival to your beauty."

Ukeko smiled at his jest but only with her lips.

"They say," Kira continued, "that your music is as beautiful as your face."

Takiko murmured a protest and tried to hide her intense discomfort by bowing her head to the mat in a show of humility.

"What do you think, my lord?" The Prince called to his brother Go Shirakawa. "Shall we have her play and judge for ourselves?"

The Retired Emperor was a tall man, with even more of an air of arrogance than his brother, as he came from the garden and climbed up into the room. "So this is the

little nightingale whom the merchant Kamaji rescued in
the wilderness?" The heavy perfume of his body stung in
Takiko's nostrils and clung to her throat. She longed to
cough but dared not. "Yes, by all means, have the pretty
child perform."

Gratefully Takiko retreated to the corner of the room
where the servants had set up her koto. She spent more
time than usual tuning the thirteen strings, needing the
extra time to calm her trembling hands. Even at that, the
first song was shaky, and she could feel the guests' rest-
lessness in the rustling of garments and hawking of
throats. But then as always the music worked its magic,
and like warm wine it invaded her bloodstream and took
her body and spirit captive. She played on and on, until
despite the chill night air she was so drenched with perspiration that it fell in great droplets upon the instrument.

"I have a poem," Go Shirakawa announced when she
had finished.

> *"The nightingale splits the darkness with her song,*
> *Even the spring moon pales at its beauty."*

"Allow me, your Majesty, the privilege of answering
your noble lines with a poor pair of my own." The request
came out of the shadows. Takiko could not see the speaker,
but she felt his presence. The quiet timber of his voice
was warm and caressing like the last chords of the ballad
she had just played. She found herself shivering.

The speaker continued:

> *"I find her chilled and trembling on the forest floor*
> *And fain would bear her gently to my nest."*

There was a silence, and then Prince Kira laughed.

"Well spoken," he cried. "Well spoken. Now more wine for everyone."

Takiko's face was fire and her body ice. The meaning of the couplet was self-evident, even a person as naive to court life as she understood the poet's intent. If she had been shivering before, now she shook all over as though she were riding in an ox cart.

"Excuse me. Forgive me," she murmured, and in the confusion of the servants' refilling the wine cups, she slipped from the room.

After a cup or two, Prince Kira noticed her absence. He motioned to one of the servants. "Where has the girl gone?" he asked in a hoarse whisper.

"She seemed tired, my lord, and begged to be excused."

The Prince frowned, and then he turned to his bride. She was a beauty, this third wife of his. He would give the little nightingale a few months to overcome her shyness, and in the meantime . . . . He smiled widely and took the wine cup Ukeko held out to him.

The next morning as Takiko combed Princess Aoi's hair, the Princess said in an offhand tone, "You are to play for the Emperor tonight. His Majesty Go Shirakawa has commanded it."

Takiko could feel her cheeks burning. Despite the honor, she had no wish to be in the presence of Go Shirakawa and his friends again, but she did not try to protest.

"You may take Mieko with you."

"Thank you, madam."

There was a long silence so quiet that the loudest noise was the sound of the comb being pulled through the Princess's hair. The shutters were closed against the cold, and the room was dark except for the flickering light of two tiny oil lamps. Once or twice the Princess sighed. Takiko wondered if she might be jealous of her husband's new wife. Her attempts to cheer the Princess when she was melancholy had all failed, so she did not try now to invade her mistress's moods.

"Tonight. After you have played for his Majesty. . . ."

"Yes, your Highness?"

"Go to the Temple of Kiyomizu."

"Yes, madam?" She waited for further instructions and when none came, she said, "What am I to do at the temple, if you please?"

"Pray," replied the Princess with a short laugh.

It was already dark outside when the carriage came to fetch the girls. Takiko was beginning to wonder if she would ever run in the sunlight again. All winter they had remained behind closed shutters, and even with spring they never seemed to leave the shadowy shell of the great house. How pale and sickly life seemed here, like a bulb shoot too long covered by leaves. On Goro's farm, even in the winter, the shutters were thrown open in the daytime for warmth and light from the sun. There one continued to go outside even in the bitterest weather, for there was work to be done and no one was permitted to hibernate. While in the spring—how she longed for the smell of green growth in the warm, wet earth! At this time and from this distance she imagined that the manure of the farm would seem more friendly to her nostrils than the heavy perfumes of Prince Kira's house.

She and Mieko climbed into the carriage and snuggled in among the quilts. The rains would begin early this year. There was an oppressive feeling in the air. Each of them put a hand on the koto to keep it from bumping about during the ride. It had been Goro's mother's, and Takiko could not bear to think of its being scratched, much less broken.

"Have you been to court before, Mieko?"

"What, me? No, never." She laughed.

Princess Aoi had given Takiko some instruction in etiquette—how to kowtow, how to address the Emperor, how to refuse refreshments—and supplied her with a few questions that might be considered appropriate conversation before she began to play. She rehearsed these now with Mieko, at first anxiously, then collapsing into nervous giggles.

"I'm so nervous."

"Oh-h, madam, with your charm?" And as usual, Mieko's flattery had a soothing effect on her, and she was able to sit a little straighter in the bumpy carriage.

Outside the curtains they could hear the challenges of gatemen, and once a guard thrust his head and shoulders between the curtains but seemed satisfied when he saw their faces by his torchlight. At last the carriage stopped, and the curtains were parted for them to alight. It was the palace. A shudder of excitement went through them both as they mounted the few stairs into the entryway. Two guards preceded them, and two followed carrying the koto. They were led down the wide wooden corridor into a large hall.

Lamps were brought and a mirror so that Mieko could comb Takiko's hair and prepare her for her presentation to the Emperor. Food was brought—and such food it was. Fresh salt-baked fish, bright oranges from the south, fragrant soup with bean curd, shrimp, and a tiny stalk of watercress for color, paper-thin slices of pink raw fish with horseradish, chicken and ginkgo nuts in hot custard, cucumbers pickled in the choicest sake, shrimp, mushrooms, tiny onions and eggplants, steaming white rice, bitter green tea, and warm, sweet wine.

"Can we eat it?" Mieko asked shyly. She still remembered the previous year's scant rations.

"I think so. It's only in the presence of his Majesty that we are forbidden to eat."

"Are you sure, madam?"

"Let's say I'm sure." Mieko giggled, and both girls fell upon the feast as wolves in winter. The aroma of the food promised no more than it gave, and though neither girl would have believed she could eat everything that had been set before her, they were embarrassed to discover that they had devoured it all. Sitting there, with her stomach too overstuffed for comfort and her eyes nearly closed, Takiko was startled by the presence of a guard asking her to present herself to the Emperor.

Mieko gave a final touch to her hair, and then they were led down the wide corridor to the Emperor's rooms.

He was seated on a pile of crimson cushions, a pale child, nodding drowsily, for the hour was late. He looked scarcely older than her brother Ichiro and far less healthy.

On either side, though a little to his rear, knelt two women. The younger woman wore the most beautiful robe that Takiko had ever seen, and at her sleeve there was the ripple of color that promised many more garments just as lovely underneath. There were jewels in the embroidery on her sash, and in her hair a comb whose jewels caught fire from the lamplight. She was, of course, the Retired Empress Kenreimon'in, whose husband Takakura had stepped aside at the age of nineteen in favor of his baby son, the boy, now scarcely five, who sat nodding on his royal pillows.

The older woman bore the shaved head and simple

dress of a nun. With a start, Takiko saw the resemblance in the two faces and realized who the nun was. Her title was now Nii no Ama, but she had once been Lady Kiyomori of the Heike. She was the widow of the great chieftain and, through her daughter, the grandmother of the little Emperor. The Senior Cloistered Emperor Go Shirakawa and his perfumed courtiers were nowhere to be seen.

It was Lady Kiyomori who spoke, leaning forward as she did so to put her hand lightly on the child's shoulder. "The koto player has come to play for your Majesty."

The boy opened his eyes and stared at Takiko wordlessly. Such large, sad eyes! She remembered in time to disengage her eyes from his and prostrate herself humbly. The little Emperor took no part in the greetings. His grandmother spoke in reply to Takiko's words of respect, and after the proper words had been said, the older woman motioned Takiko to her instrument and indicated that she was to begin.

Takiko began with a ballad, one that always drew praise, but she soon realized the child was bored with it, so she cut three stanzas and brought it quickly to an end. The nun's forehead wrinkled—she evidently knew the ballad—but she did not protest.

"When the world was young, the King of the Dragons who lived at the source of the sun, decided to take for himself a bride." Takiko began to sing. The boy opened his half-shut eyes. "So he chose for himself a beautiful young girl dragon, and they were married with great joy and feasting and drinking before the sacred shrine."

The tune was a lively one and Takiko could not help smiling at the boy as she sang. "But alas, his great happiness was cut short when his beautiful young bride fell ill with a disease that no physician could cure and he was afraid she would die.

" 'Oh, my darling, my beautiful dragon,' the Dragon King wept. 'What shall I do to save you?' And he wept great dragon tears causing the ocean to rise and flood the eastern provinces. 'There is only one thing that will save me,' his queen replied. 'You must get for me the liver of a monkey. Only this will make me well.' 'But, my dear,' replied the Dragon King, 'you know as well as I do that we live in the depths of the ocean. There are no monkeys here.'

"And now it was the Dragon Queen who wept great dragon tears causing another flood to rise in the eastern provinces. 'Boohoo! Boohoo! You love me not!' 'My dearest one, I love you more than my life!' 'Then you will find me a monkey liver!' she demanded.

"The Dragon King called for his most trusted retainer, the jellyfish. 'Go, jellyfish, and fetch me a monkey, for my wife must have his liver else she dies.'

"Now the jellyfish did as he was told. He swam as near as he could to the shore until he found a monkey sitting on a large rock high above the flood. 'Oh, Mr. Monkey,' he called. 'Come away with me under the sea to Dragon Land and feast on fresh melons and sleep in a silken bed.'

"To the monkey who was cold and hungry this sounded very inviting, so he hopped on the back of the jellyfish and they started back to Dragon Land."

The Emperor was wide awake now, his head forward, listening intently to the tale. Takiko smiled at the boy; she could not fear him, Emperor though he was, when he loved a children's song so much. "And then what happened?" he cried out.

"And then, and then," she sang. "The monkey began to be afraid. Perhaps the jellyfish is tricking me, he thought, and when they were so far out at sea that they could no longer see the land, he said, 'Tell me, Mr. Jellyfish, why did you choose *me* for this great honor in Dragon Land? There are many other worthy creatures you might have invited.'

" 'Ah, but none,' answered the foolish jellyfish, 'none who have a monkey's liver. And it is that which my master must have to cure his ailing Queen.'

" 'Why didn't you tell me? There is nothing that would give me greater joy than to serve their Majesties, but I left my liver behind, hanging in the branches of a great chestnut tree. It's very heavy, a liver is, so I usually take it off when I'm hunting for food. Now we must go all the way back and get it.' "

The Emperor smiled at these clever words.

"So the jellyfish took the monkey all the way back to shore, all the way to where a giant chestnut tree spread its branches over the water. The monkey jumped off the jellyfish's back and climbed to the top of the tree. 'Alas, my brother,' he called down, 'while we were gone, someone has come and stolen my liver. I will make a diligent search for it, but you, meantime, go back and tell the Dragon King what has happened, and meet me here again in the morning.'

"Thus the jellyfish returned to his master without the monkey and told the King what had happened. The Dragon King cried out in rage: 'You foolish stupid thing! You have allowed that wicked monkey to outwit you. Now my beautiful wife will die!' And he was so angry that he took a stick and beat the jellyfish until he had broken every bone in his body. Which is why to this day jellyfish are just a mass of jelly."

"But the Dragon Queen," protested the child. "Did she die?"

Takiko laughed and continued. "The Dragon Queen rose from her sickbed to see what all the ruckus was about. And when the desolate King told her that there was no monkey liver to make her well, she said: 'Then I'll just have to get well without it.' And she did."

The boy clapped his hands. "Sing it again," he begged. And Takiko did—two more times. Then she sang other songs—of Momotaro, the boy who was born out of a peach and who with his companions, a dog, a monkey, and a pheasant conquered a whole island of giants; of the day the Gods teased the Sun Goddess out of hiding to return light to the world; and of Urashima, the fisherman, who married the Dragon King's daughter and lived for four hundred years under the Deep Sea.

Then because it was so late, Takiko began to sing gentle songs and even country lullabies that she had learned from Fusa. Lady Kiyomori took the child in her arms, and soon he was fast asleep. "You have given us much pleasure," she whispered.

"I fear I forgot my place, your Holiness. I have a little brother, so . . . ."

"Sometimes"—the nun spoke softly—"we wish his Highness might be a little boy." A lady-in-waiting came to take the sleeping Emperor from her arms, but the nun shook her head. "Give me your hand, Takiko," she said. Takiko put out her hand, and the older woman pulled herself to her feet, still carrying the child.

"Let me hold him, Mother. He is heavy for you." The young Empress spoke for the first time. And, indeed on her feet, the tiny woman seemed too frail for even the weight of such a slender boy. But again the nun shook her head. "I am strong, my daughter, too strong for a woman, they say." She smiled at Takiko. "Good night, pretty child. Go in health."

When Takiko and Mieko climbed into their carriage, it was well past midnight. They both fell asleep among the quilts as the oxen bumped along through the silent streets. Takiko was abruptly aware of a rough male voice. The carriage had stopped.

"Are we home, Mieko?"

Mieko stuck her head out of the curtains and spoke to one of the retainers.

"We seem to be at Kiyomizu Temple."

"Kiyomizu? Why have we come here?"

"On your order, madam."

Sleepily Takiko retraced the long evening until she remembered the command she herself had given the attendant hours earlier. She had not thought of Princess Aoi's strange demand all evening. She was to come to Kiyomizu and pray. Well, she was here, though she had no notion of what she was to pray for.

She crossed the dark temple courtyard following the chief carriage attendant, with Mieko at her heels. They were met at the entrance by a shaven-headed boy carrying an oil lamp who inquired their business.

"I am lady-in-waiting to Princess Aoi, and I have come to pray." Takiko imitated the Princess's imperious tones, which made this midnight pilgrimage sound almost reasonable.

The boy led them to a small chamber where he lighted candles before the image. Takiko knelt down, her body in an attitude of prayer but her mind a tangle of confusion. It was obvious that the Princess had entrusted her with some mission, but how was she to perform it when she had been told nothing about it? Every limb longed for bed and sleep, and she was afraid to close her eyes for fear she would fall asleep on the spot.

Mieko was kneeling beside her, and Takiko could see from the corner of her eye the girl's head dangerously bobbing on her shoulders. She was debating the wisdom of poking Mieko when a low masculine voice just behind her said: "So the Princess trusts only you, little nightingale."

It was a voice she knew but she could not remember where she had heard it. She did not know whether she should turn to face the speaker or not, so she remained motionless. The man came and seated himself between her and the altar. His knees nearly touched her own.

In the candlelight she could see his young, lean face. His eyes shone with mirth. His nose was perhaps a trifle too long for perfection, but the effect was enough to make a young girl catch her breath. He wore the robe of a monk, but the hood had fallen from his head to reveal not the shaved head of a priest but the topknot of a samurai. He put a long-fingered hand on her knee.

"You are trembling, little one." It was then that she remembered where she had heard his voice—in the blackness of Prince Kira's garden. His hand burned through the twelve layers of her garments. Her heart seemed about to crash through her breast, and her throat was so dry she could not speak. She slipped out from under his hand and cleared her throat.

"I have come on an errand for my lady."

He smiled but did not try to touch her again. Instead he leaned close to her and whispered. "Tell your mistress that Munemori was disastrously defeated—" Takiko gasped, but he seemed not to notice it.

"And that I go now to join Yoshitsune as I promised.

I shall not see her again until the sons of Yoshitomo of the Genji come in victory."

He was her enemy, a spy of the Genji against her people in the city. He was also, without doubt, her mistress's lover, and yet, and yet, she wished he would put his hand upon her knee again. But he did not. Instead he opened his mouth in a wide smile, showing two rows of perfect teeth. How different he was from the men of the court with their fat faces and stifling perfume. He had a warm mannish odor, not of clay and animals like Goro, but of clean healthy skin.

"I will convey your message only to my mistress."

"There's a pretty girl." He rose to go.

"And —"

"Yes?" He turned.

"Bear yourself carefully." She blushed furiously, a fact that the candlelight did not altogether hide.

"And you, little nightingale. Go in health." He pulled up the hood of his robe and was gone.

"He liked you." Mieko spoke for the first time.

"What nonsense!" Her reply sounded crosser than she meant it to.

She awoke in the middle of the night with a feeling she could not name — a mixture of pain and sweetness. A hand upon her knee. *He is my enemy. My mistress's lover. I don't even know his name.* And she turned and wept, the tears running down the side of her wooden pillow into the quilt.

SEVEN
The Flight

"Her Majesty was pleased with you last night." It was the first thing Princess Aoi had said during the morning hair combing. Other servants bustled about, refilling the braziers with fresh coals. It had begun to rain during the night, and the house was unpleasantly damp. There had been no chance to deliver the samurai's message.

"Her Majesty is kind."

"No, actually, unkind." Aoi said sharply. "She wants to steal you from me!"

Takiko kept combing rhythmically, but her mind was a jumble.

"Well, what do you say?"

"I, madam? I hardly know . . . I did not expect."

"Nor did I. Or I would never have let you go to the

palace last night." There was a petulant note in the Princess's voice. "She's as stubborn as her father, old Kiyomori. I don't begrudge them the kingdom, but I do resent their snatching my best hairdresser."

The word "kingdom" brought last night's message sharply into focus. She bent close to her mistress's ear. "I have a message, madam."

Aoi's eyes brightened. "Out, out, all of you! What turtles you are this morning!" She clapped her hands in impatience, and the servants were soon out of sight. Takiko knew better than to hope that they were all out of hearing—paper doors and silken screens invited curious ears the way day-old fish wooed cats.

She bent close to the gleaming black head and whispered, "Munemori is defeated."

Aoi gave a curious smile. "No? The fat goose! And the gentleman?"

"He—he goes to join Yoshitsune."

Aoi's face fell. "He will come again?" She asked in a careless tone, but Takiko could feel the tension beneath the question.

"He said to tell you"—how painful to repeat these words—"that he will come in triumph."

Princess Aoi turned away. "Tell me, Takiko. Do you find me ugly?"

"Ugly, madam? Oh, no. You are very beautiful."

"Old, then?"

"No, my lady, not at all."

"Young men have sharp eyes. So sharp. Oh, Hideo"—her voice was a whisper—"are you tired so soon?" A sigh shook her body. Then after a silence she said aloud, "Do not love a man, Takiko. Love is too cruel."

It was advice the girl had heard before, but now it was too late. She loved. And already she knew how cruel it was. But at least, although unwittingly, her mistress had given her a great gift. She had told her his name. *Hideo*, *Hideo*, *Hideo*, Takiko repeated it over and over within herself, and her heart beat painfully against her breast, and her knee burned.

"Well, what shall I tell her Majesty?"

"I'm—I'm sorry, madam?"

"Will you be going to the palace?"

"I don't know. What should I do, madam? I have no wish to leave you," she said, which was not entirely true. She would be glad to be free of what she felt to be a threat from Prince Kira and her jealousy now of the Princess. And yet, if she left, she might never hear of Hideo again.

"I don't know. I suppose there's nothing to be done. At least for now," Aoi said snappishly. "Go Shirakawa has too much power, and she is his son's wife and the sister of General Munemori; the devil take her." She admired her hair in the hand mirror. "I must consult a diviner. Such a streak of bad luck." She examined her blackened teeth. "Well, go on. You'll need new clothes, but her Highness can provide those herself. I won't let her take complete advantage of me. That mother of hers is behind it, I'll wager. Why doesn't she go back to the nunnery where she belongs?"

Takiko bowed. "I am deeply indebted to you for all your kindnesses to me."

"Yes, well . . . ." She waved her hand in dismissal.

"Could I? Would it be possible for Mieko to go with me?"

"Yes, yes. Take anyone you like."

"Will you tell my parents where I am?"

"They will be told."

"Thank you, madam. You are very kind. I hope I shall be seeing you again."

"Not likely. Well, off you go." Takiko bowed again at the door. "I'll miss you," Aoi said, her tone as sharp as when she had cursed the Empress.

Takiko and Mieko settled into the palace routine with surprising ease. Takiko was no longer in demand as a hairdresser. She was to be available to play the koto and sing when called upon. The Retired Empress Kenreimon'in discovered that she could read Chinese characters, so every morning she was summoned to read poetry for the Empress and her ladies. Lady Kiyomori, shaved and in her humble attire, was always in evidence, like a falcon among peacocks. The young Emperor had tutors, of course, but he much preferred Takiko's playful company, so she would often help him with simple characters. He was only five, and although a great show was made of his education, at the moment no one took it very seriously.

By this time the news of Munemori's defeat was known. When the Heike nobles dared think of it, dread beat on their hearts like the relentless summer rains. No one knew just what the defeat might mean, but no one was prepared for what actually happened.

"Wake up, madam! Wake up!" Mieko was pushing her roughly and almost shouting.

"What is it?"

"Munemori. He is here." Takiko sat up in bed, fully awake now.

"What's happening?"

At that moment Lady Kiyomori herself burst into the room. "Will you go with us?"

"Madam, what is it?" Takiko leaped out from under the quilts to do obeisance.

"There is no time. We leave in an hour."

"Where are we going, your Holiness?"

"Munemori is taking the Emperor south to escape the Genji. His mother and I will go. We will take the Emperor's younger brother and whichever of her ladies is willing—" A man's voice from the corridor shouted for speed.

"The Empress will not order you to go, Takiko. This is not your war. I am the wife of Kiyomori, and she is his daughter. No one wonders where our loyalties lie, but you belong to neither clan so . . . ."

"No, madam, I am a Heike. My father was Moriyuki. He died for your husband's cause, and I am not afraid to do as much."

The nun smiled. "No one is talking of dying, my pretty child. Though exile is a kind of death. But, thank you. I knew your father in the old days. He would be proud of you."

There was another shout from the hall and the sound of feet running through the corridors. Lady Kiyomori left to see about the little Emperor. Takiko dressed herself while Mieko made a bundle of their clothes. They decided to take a mirror and leave the koto—only because it was so awkward to carry. As frightened as they both were, there was something undeniably exciting about it all. Takiko began to compose a ballad in her head about the midnight kidnaping of the Emperor and the beautiful ladies that followed him into hiding. She would miss her koto.

As they came out of the palace, they saw a great light in the eastern sky. "It is Rokuhara," Mieko whispered. "The Heike are burning it so that Yoshinaka will not get the chance." Rokuhara—Kiyomori's glory turned to ashes.

The soldiers escorted the girls into a carriage with two other ladies-in-waiting, and before they were really settled, the carriage moved off with a lurch, throwing the four of them into a jumbled heap at the rear. Takiko began to laugh, as she disentangled her sleeves from around Mieko's neck.

"Quiet, you silly girl. Don't you realize what's happening?" Lady Chujo, the older of the two ladies-in-waiting, said sternly.

"Yes. I'm sorry."

"We may never see the capital again, you know."

If Mieko and Takiko had had any thought of chattering and giggling to pass the weary hours, the presence of Lady Chujo kept them from it. The unfortunate lady was famous for two things—her piety and her ugliness. She had been cursed with a huge bulbous nose, which would have seemed much more at home on a tavern-keeper than a lady of noble birth. She bore this burden with utmost dignity, and the time other women spent before their mirrors or with their lovers she occupied in telling her prayer beads, lest, as some court wags would have it, she might be reincarnated in some future life as a *tengu*, with a nose as long as her feet.

Sometimes she prayed silently and sometimes she prayed audibly, but always she prayed, so that one might have thought that it was her large fingers upon the beads that kept the carriage jerking forward rather than the plodding of two oxen.

Takiko would have minded much more being imprisoned in the tiny carriage with such a person, had not her mind a theme it delighted to embroider. She took the figure of the young samurai whom, to be sure, she had seen only once and that in candlelight and began to imagine him in every sort of scene. Eating, riding, playing football (how strong and skillful he was!), listening in the shadows as someone (herself, perhaps) played the koto. She would not picture him even speaking to a woman — an attempt, no doubt, to keep out a vision of him with Aoi. The longer the journey became, the closer he came to seeing her, until giving herself up completely to her passion, she imagined the love note he might send, her delicate reply, an oblique conversation with the screen between them, and at last the night when he would climb silently into her open window. . . .

At various times during the day they were permitted to alight from the carriage for a few minutes and stretch their sore limbs while the oxen were watered and fed. Sometimes during the night Takiko would wake up and realize the caravan had stopped. Even Munemori realized that he would kill the beasts if he gave them no rest. But from the direction of the sun Takiko could tell that they were pushing westward as fast as possible. If war-horses were in pursuit, it was unlikely that the oxen could long escape them, but no war-horses appeared, so it seemed that the Genji had been content for the present to capture the city and let the Emperor go.

"But then, of course, my lord Go Shirakawa has got himself another Emperor by now." The speaker was Lady Midori, the fourth member of their party.

"He wouldn't dare!" Takiko was trying to hop out a leg cramp during their stop when Lady Midori made this observation.

"Don't be silly. There are plenty of grandsons left in the capital whose mothers are not Heike. He'll just install one of them."

"He can't." Lady Chujo's sepulchral voice joined the conversation.

"Who's to stop him? Lord Kiyomori is dead and won't argue with him this time. The Genji won't be clever enough even to argue. He's certainly not hesitated to play the god before. Why should he now?"

"Before," intoned the grand lady, "before he had the Royal treasures. Not even Go Shirakawa can appoint an Emperor without the sword, the jewel, and the mirror."

"What do you mean? Where are the Imperial Regalia now?" Takiko asked.

"There." Lady Chujo flung a long arm out and pointed to the carriage of Lady Kiyomori.

Takiko smiled in admiration of the little nun. "Isn't she brave? And clever?"

"Brave, yes. But clever? Now the Genji will have to pursue us whether they have the stomach for it or not. Her bravado may cost us all our lives."

"Don't be morbid, Chujo. The girl is right. We should admire her Holiness."

Lady Chujo extracted her beads from her belt as though to ward off the evil folly surrounding her. With a sigh she began to mumble her prayers as they climbed back into the carriage and the journey began again.

Many days and prayers later, though Takiko would have been at a loss to say just how many, the caravan came to a halt. They had come at last to the sea, opposite the island of Kyushu.

As they left the mainland in tiny boats, soldiers standing guard on the decks, Takiko began to realize, perhaps for the first time, what this exile might mean. She had not even been able to send word to her mother and Goro that she had left the capital, though Princess

Aoi had said she would let them know that Takiko was joining the Empress's household. But even if they knew that, they would not know where she was now. She might never see them again. Homesickness grasped her in a cold embrace. *Dear, dear Fusa, I will never help you cook again or go mushroom picking in the woods. You will weep for me, I know. But Ichiro—I will only be a name to you; you will not remember that you ever knew me. Mother—how often I hurt you with my childish obstinacy. And Goro, my monkey father.* She had not known that she loved him.

EIGHT
The Devil's Horsemen

To say that Yoshinaka entered the capital without bloodshed is not to say that he took it without struggle. For the Retired Emperor Go Shirakawa, with the weakened Heike out of the way, was on the verge of satisfying his enormous appetite for power. He had no intention of allowing the mere cousin of the Genji chieftain to snatch it from him before he took the first taste.

There was the matter of appointing a new Emperor. As the new military dictator of the city, Yoshinaka had quite naturally assumed that it was his privilege, as it had once been Kiyomori's, to choose the occupant for the throne. But the wily Go Shirakawa, while pretending to bow to the commander's every wish, suddenly made the public announcement that his four-year-old grandson Go Toba was to be the new Emperor.

Yoshinaka was enraged. There was nothing he could do. The old Retired Emperor's power over the people was too strong simply to set aside Go Shirakawa's choice once it had been proclaimed. But in revenge, Yoshinaka loosed his troops from all restraint, and the fierce mountain men fell upon the helpless city like a human plague, pillaging, burning, looting, raping.

Go Shirakawa sent a messenger to the only man in Japan who could save the city — Yoritomo, chief of the Genji.

No word of Takiko had reached Goro's household since before the defeat of Munemori. On the farm they had watched the movement of troops toward the city and had suffered the confiscation of rice and meat first by the retreating Heike and then by Yoshinaka's advancing Genji.

At Chieko's pleading, Goro himself went to the city to find Takiko and bring her home, at least until the troubles were over. To his dismay he came to a city in flames, and though he fought his way through the debris and smoke to the house where he believed her to be living, no one there could give him news of the girl other than the vague comfort that when last seen she had been alive and well. And, oh, yes, almost as an afterthought, hadn't she gone to live in the palace just a few days before the troubles began?

He made his way to the north-central section of the city, which was cordoned off by Genji guardsmen. With the aid of a considerable bribe he was allowed to approach the palace, and with the lubricant of more and more coins he eventually found a maid who had known Takiko and who whispered that she had been among the Emperor's party that Munemori had forced to accompany him in his retreat. The little maid took him to Takiko's old quarters where the only familiar sign that she had ever been there was her koto, carefully wrapped in brocade. He bound it up in a bed quilt and tied it with cords that the maid found for him. The length of it was taller than his height, but he swung it awkwardly on his wide shoulder and carried it home, where Fusa and Chieko wept over it as though it were Takiko's body he had brought.

Takiko herself, however, had hardly felt more alive since she left Goro's household. After some initial mis-calculations, Munemori had at last found a haven on the island of Yashima, off Shikoku, where the local chiefs were not adverse to the presence in their midst of a deposed boy Emperor and a hapless Heike general with their entourage. Here the party was free to move about, both indoors and outside, and though most of the noble ladies kept to themselves, Takiko was happy to be in the country again, and she and Mieko made friends with the farmers nearby. They even helped harvest the oranges, staining their silk robes with the fresh juice while delighting in the smell and flavor of the golden balls.

One day the two of them with Emperor Antoku in tow were sitting by the bank of the creek which ran past the orchard, drawing characters in the dirt in the sort of lessons the three of them took pleasure in when, with a little cry, Takiko made her stick go deeper and deeper into the soil. Then much to the others' amazement she began to dig with her fingertips until she had dug up a goose-egg size of earth.

"It's clay!" she exclaimed joyfully.

"And so?" Mieko asked.

"We can make things from it." She dug up more for

each of them, and the poetry lesson turned into a pottery session like the ones she had had so long ago with Goro.

For a few days they were content to press the clay with their fingers into animal and human shapes to show the Emperor's little brother and even into the form of vessels that they let bake in the sun. But when Takiko told the Emperor about Goro's wheel, he was determined to have one, so Takiko explained to a farmer friend how Goro's had been made. After several disappointing attempts, he at last succeeded in making one for them, which though not as delicately balanced as Goro's, worked reasonably well.

Meantime, Takiko showed Antoku and Mieko how to pick out all the imperfections from the clay that might destroy a vessel on the wheel. They took turns beating the clay with stones, and then, finally, Takiko, like the chief cook of the Imperial Palace, added just that exact amount of water that she as the master knew to be necessary.

The other two used the wheel as one plays a favorite sport with humor and enthusiasm, but they soon became aware that for Takiko it was not a game.

Somehow as she whirled the wheel and brought clay to life upon it, she was binding herself again to Goro's household and all that she loved there. She drove herself as Goro had never tried to, striving to perfect the most delicate forms. Never did she allow herself the luxury of quitting in exasperation as she had when she was with Goro. "When I see him again he will marvel at how much I have learned," she promised herself. Only when the Emperor grasped her arm and pulled her away would she leave the wheel for other amusements.

Try as she would she could think of no way to provide herself with a kiln. She was sure there was some secret to the way one was built—else why had Goro sent to Korea for a craftsman to build his? So though it chafed her, she had to be content simply to let the sun bake her pottery. Sometimes she would try to stain it with berry juices or the purple dye of the Awa district instead of a glaze, but these did not satisfy her.

She had a mirror, so she knew that life outdoors was changing her looks. She and Mieko always took care to wear hats against the sun to keep their skin white and soft, but the hats did not keep the sun from reaching inside her body and giving her cheeks a glow of health. Sometimes she wished as Mieko combed her hair that Hideo might see her now, but she had to dismiss the thought as disloyal, for she would only see Hideo if Heike and Genji met again in battle, and she knew Munemori was not ready.

The Lady Kiyomori also had a mirror—the sacred mirror that Amaterasu, the Goddess of the Sun, was said to have given to her grandson, Ninigi, the first Emperor. It was kept in a carved wooden chest that no one dared to open, for to look upon the sacred mirror would be to see what no mere human eye could bear to look upon. Lady Kiyomori carried in a second wooden chest that curiously curved jewel that once had adorned the sacred mirror, and finally the ancient sword that the Storm God, Susano, had pulled from the tail of the Dragon of Koshi and that he had given to Amaterasu in apology for mischief he had caused her.

These three—the mirror, the jewel, and the sword—formed the Imperial Regalia without which no Emperor could be crowned. Lady Kiyomori had taken them to protect the throne for Antoku, her beloved grandson and the grandson of Heike no Kiyomori.

Munemori was encouraged. In their time on Yashima, away from the luxuries of the city, his troops were beginning to grow hardened. They were able to persuade some of the chieftains of the neighboring island of Shikoku to assist their cause, and word came from the mainland that still others would join them there. The Genji were being weakened by continuous struggles for power. When spies brought news that Yoshitsune, Yoritomo's youngest brother, had been dispatched to the capital to destroy the forces of his cousin Yoshinaka, Munemori felt that the time to return to the mainland had come. An advance force of four thousand men was sent on the two days' journey by boat to Settsu Province. There, along the narrow beach between Ichinotani and Fukuwara, the soldiers began building what Munemori envisioned as an impregnable base. The sea that the Heike had sailed fearlessly since the days when Kiyomori's father, old Tadamori, had pursued pirates for profit and glory, the sea that the Genji neither knew nor trusted, lay before them, and rising sheer from the beach at Ichinotani were the impassable mountains. The beach was narrow. It would be easy to repulse any attacks upon his flanks.

Just as Munemori was preparing to transfer the remainder of his men, including the Emperor's party, to the new fortifications, an envoy arrived from Go Shirakawa. The Retired Emperor wished to share with the honored chieftain of the Heike the news that General Yoshitsune of the Genji was now in complete military control of the capital, having been sent by his brother, Yoritomo of the Genji, to destroy their treacherous cousin, the late General Yoshinaka, whose headless bones were now picked clean by the hungry birds of winter. The Genji were in complete harmony now, and Yoritomo was their undisputed chieftain.

It was therefore his desire, indeed his command as Senior Cloistered Emperor, and the desire and command of Yoritomo, military commander of all Japan, that Munemori repent of his foolish rebellion against the throne and return to the capital, bringing with him the young deposed Emperor and the Imperial Regalia — jewel, mirror, and sword.

If the honorable Munemori would obey this order by the second day of March, a truce between the warring clans could be arranged through the gracious offices of his Imperial Majesty, the Senior Cloistered Emperor. If — the Gods forbid — Munemori should be so foolish or ungrateful as to refuse this offer, the brilliant General Yoshitsune with the whole force of the Genji army would sweep the beaches of Yashima like a tidal wave leaving no trace of what it had destroyed.

Now it has been said that of the sons of Kiyomori, Munemori was the least intelligent, but even a clam flees the courtship of the octopus. Although the fortifications at Ichinotani were not quite complete, he set sail at once. And fearing the men who had come as envoys would return as spies, he bound them without ceremony and took them along.

The March wind that blew upon the Heike fleet was cold and capricious. Most of the nobles languished below deck. But Takiko and Mieko knelt behind the railing near the prow of the ship, just their eyes and noses above the bamboo slatwork. The small vessel rose and fell, smacking the white waves with such force that often it sent the two of them rolling across the deck. If the girls had known the power of the sea, they might have been afraid, but this was only their third voyage and the first two, from the mainland to Kyushu, then from Kyushu to Yashima, they had been kept in the cabin. Never before had they been drenched by the waves nor had their nostrils been assaulted by the smell of salt and sea life. They clung to each other laughing with the joy of losing their small spirits into the enormous presence of the sea.

"Let's get the Emperor!" Takiko cried above the noise of the waves.

The two girls slid and fell to the entrance of the deck cabin where a smiling guard helped them pry open the door and held it for them as they tumbled in.

"Where have you foolish girls been?" Lady Chujo looked down her long nose in horror.

In the stuffy cabin with every royal eye upon them, Takiko suddenly felt her hair sticky with salt and the clamminess of her silk robes against her skin, but she did not want Lady Chujo to know she felt ashamed, so she said quietly, "We have been watching the sea."

"And isn't it magnificent?" It was Lady Kiyomori. Like the grandmother that she was, she led the soaking girls to a corner of the cabin and helped them change their garments.

Lady Midori came forward to help, but the little nun waved her away. "This hair!" she said in mock exasperation. "Bring me a damp cloth, Lady Chujo." The lady's face flushed, but she moved to obey. "We can't wash it here, but we'll do the best we can. Here—" She took the cloth from Lady Chujo and began to wipe first Takiko's and then Mieko's hair. Both girls and the other ladies of the court tried to protest the grand lady's actions, but she was like a mother cat licking her kittens and would not be distracted from her task.

"Now," she sighed, when at last she had satisfied herself that she could do no more, "why don't you sing for us, little Takiko?" She took the Emperor upon her lap and the Empress held her younger son on hers. The ladies of the court settled themselves as comfortably as they could upon a tilting floor.

Takiko had no instrument, but her voice was true and strong:

> *"From the land of golden oranges,*
> *Homeward we come*
> *On the Dragon King's rippling back.*
> *It is spring.*
> *Our hearts are eager as her first green shoots.*
> *It is morning;*
> *Our flag is red as rays of the rising sun."*

There was a murmur of approval.

"Our flag is red as the drops of tomorrow's blood." The words, which must have come from Lady Chujo, sent a chill through Takiko, but everyone pretended that nothing had been said.

Munemori's warship was next to their own, and in the morning the Emperor's party watched the general take a small boat into the shore to inspect the fortifications. They had been cramped into the confines of the small cabin for nearly two days, and they had been in exile for more than seven months, so they were anxious to feel the dry land of the mainland under their feet once more. To their disappointment, Munemori returned at noon to report that quarters for the Emperor and his party were not yet completed and they would have to spend at least one night at anchor in the bay.

Takiko wished that the Empress or Lady Kiyomori would ask for enough fresh water for bathing and hair washing, but they did not, and she was hesitant to. She had no one but herself to blame for her sticky hair and the dried sea water prickling at her skin.

But the one night they were to spend at anchor became two, then three, then four, and all the women began to complain. They would far rather stay in primitive arrangements on the beach than remain another night in the stifling cabin.

Lady Chujo dictated a formal protest to the general which Takiko, being the only real scribe among them, penned and folded for formal delivery.

It was never sent.

For on the night of March eighteenth, Yoshitsune attacked a small Heike patrol force, and the battle of Ichinotani began.

The Heike troops waited almost eagerly for the next enemy move. They felt sure that theirs was the larger army and that their position was secure. The mountains protected their rear, and before them was a great fleet of warships flying the red flag of the Heike. Yoshitsune might be a wily general, but he was neither a bird that he could fly over the cliffs nor a fish that he could come at them from under the sea.

There was no sign of the white flags of the Genji all that day. From Ichinotani on the west to Ikuta Woods on the east, five thousand Heike waited, listening, watching. There were two directions from which Yoshitsune might come: from the west, striking the western flank at Ichinotani or from the east, striking the force at Ikuta Woods.

Sea gulls called to each other, swooping down upon hapless fish in the bay. And the Heike waited.

The sun set behind the mountains, and still the only sounds were the cries of the night birds and the lapping of the waves upon the shore. No one slept on the beach, and on the warship only the children, and they fitfully.

At dawn the warriors came, screaming their terrible cries from the east, their thundering war-horses crashing through Ikuta Woods, and from the west galloping toward the fortifications at Ichinotani.

From the ship it looked to Takiko like a giant picture scroll come to life. She could hear the cries of battle and the whinnying of the war-horses, but they were removed and fascinating, flashes of brilliant color upon the silken sand, as the white flags of the Genji pushed in toward the red flags of the Heike. The mountain rose sheer behind, dotted here and there with the green of a hearty scrub pine and crowned above with a thick patchwork in shades of green and brown.

"They're falling back!" Lady Chujo had grabbed Takiko's sleeve. Takiko looked up in annoyance. The woman's ugly face was twitching agitatedly.

"Only to the east. Look at Ichinotani—at the earth-works. The Genji are getting nowhere. That's where Munemori has put the real strength. They'll never get past the earthworks. It's probably a trick to draw the enemy closer to the earthworks where our archers can destroy them." She was conscious as she spoke that she was parroting tales of battle she had heard from her father years ago. But she was not displeased with their effect on the women around her on the deck. Even Lady Chujo fell silent except for an occasional nervous sniff of her famous nose.

As the sun rose higher, the Heike fell back, horseman by horseman, from their position at Ikuta Woods. Reserves were sent up, but if this threw doubt on Takiko's theory of the battle plan, no one spoke of it. The tide lapped the small boats anchored on the beach. The cries of battle seemed more muted as the first fury settled into the work of war.

But then, *"Eiiii! Eiiii!"*

It sounded like the cry of some terrible bird of prey there on the ridge of the mountain, rising from its nest with a burst of color. For a moment the battle came to a halt, and every eye turned to stare—even those who had expected it—waited for it. It was Yoshitsune and a band of Genji horsemen plunging down the cliff like a multicolored waterfall roaring and thundering over its crest, crashing upon the rocks below.

In a few terrible moments they were within the earthworks, horses rearing, swords clashing. With a great burst of energy, the Genji to the east and the west pushed back the dumbstruck and devastated Heike.

The camp was now ablaze. One of Yoshitsune's horsemen had been dispatched to that task. The day was lost.

Munemori ordered retreat, and those who could, boarded the small boats and pushed out from the bloody sands.

"Get below! Get below!" the captain bellowed. The fear-stricken women herded the children back into the tiny cabin. No one spoke as anchor was weighed and they set sail once more for Yashima. Other warships would go closer into the harbor, but this ship bore the Emperor and the Imperial Regalia and must make for safety with all possible speed.

"Thank the merciful Kwannon that Yoshitsune has no ships," Lady Kiyomori said more to herself than to the others crowded upon the floor of the tiny cabin. There was no answer, only the heavy breathing of wild creatures driven back into the uncertain safety of their den.

Lady Chujo broke the silence with the clacking of prayer beads and calls to prayer. Several of the women joined her in the mumbled chanting of the sutras, but

Takiko sat alone in the corner with her eyes closed, trying to still the thousand screaming voices within herself.
Most of all, that one voice which kept saying: "He was
one of them. Hideo was one of those terrible horsemen
who flew down the mountainside as though on the back
of the War God." As though spewn from the mouth of
Heaven—or Hell. Were they Gods or demons? How awful
they were, how magnificent!

At last, she too joined the chanting—louder than
anyone else. If she could not still the storm music of her
traitorous heart, she would drown it in prayer.

NINE

The Cry of the Nightingale

Spring came as spring always does in a burst of promises. The fields about the manor where the exiled court lived were a fuzz of green; the plum blossoms had long fallen; but there were the whites and pinks of the cherry trees, the purple blossoms of the *kiri,* and the yellow of the *keyaki.* Then came the wisteria, falling in white and violet showers from the trellises about the house, filling the air with its melancholy sweetness.

It filled Takiko's nostrils and sent through her body a great shudder of pity for her clan, her family, and herself. How could the earth be so beautiful and life so painful?

Another emissary arrived from Go Shirakawa. This time the message was sent under the name of Shigehira, one of the hapless officers of the Heike at Ikuta Woods, who was now a prisoner of war in the capital: *Bring back the Emperor; bring back the Imperial Regalia.*

Munemori replied by sending reinforcements to his troops at Hikoshima and to the Heike scattered along the shore of the southern tip of the mainland. He would control the sea; for as long as he did, no Genji could defeat him.

Summer came, and with it the rains. In the fields, the peasants of Yashima bent, ankle-deep in muddy water, to transplant into the paddies the new rice shoots. Even when the rain stopped briefly, it hung in the air, warm and ominous. The wooden shutters of the house were usually closed even in the daytime to keep out the rain and the poisonous vapors which the rain brought with it. The ladies of the court drank barley tea, and changed their damp garments and bedding as often as they could, but nothing was really dry, and the smell of the mold and mildew seemed to be everywhere — in the very rice they ate, as well as in their clothes and beds.

The little Emperor, never healthy, came down with a terrible cold. Lady Kiyomori made rice gruel for him with her own hands. And his mother, Empress Kenreimon'in, held him in her arms and tried to still the dreadful hacking cough that echoed through the women's quarters.

"It's the wasting sickness," Lady Chujo said.

"Nonsense," Takiko said it sharply to deny her own fears. "His Majesty has a cold. When the sun returns . . . ."

And the sun did return. Fields of rape caught yellow fire, and the green rice bowed under the weight of a full harvest. Winter, thought Takiko, as she and Mieko ran to the willow spring, winter can be borne, but the rains — who can bear such a weight of gloom? She stretched her hands up to the sun blindingly bright against the blue sky. Oh, Amaterasu, why do you hide yourself from us? But when Mieko asked what she was doing, she dropped her hands and replied, "Nothing."

The Emperor improved, but only a little. Sometimes Lady Kiyomori or Empress Kenreimon'in carried him into the sunlight for a few minutes, but there was no running to the spring or the creek bank with the girls to study Chinese or make pottery. He was thinner than ever, and one cough would shake his tiny frame like wind in willow branches. He had no energy and spent most of his time propped up on his bedding, his eyes dull, hardly turning his head when someone spoke to him.

One day Mieko said to Takiko, "If only you had your koto. He used to love to hear you play." This remark emboldened Takiko to broach the matter to Lady Kiyomori, who needed no courage to tell her son, General Munemori, to get a koto—the sound of which might be more beneficial to his little Majesty than the finest herbs.

It took more than a month for the instrument to arrive, but it was greeted by the whole court with great rejoicing. The women pressed about as Takiko tuned it. It did not have quite the rich tone of her own koto—the one Goro had given her—but it was as good as the one on which Lady Uchinaka had taught her to play, and so thrilled was she to have once again the thirteen strings beneath her hands that she forgave its lack of perfection.

She finished the tuning. The crowd pushed back a respectful distance while she attached the plectrums to her fingers. She held her hand high above the strings for a moment, savoring the court's anticipation. Then she brought it down in a crash with a drinking song of the foot soldiers. There was a burst of surprised laughter, and then quickly they all recovered and sang loudly the bawdy chorus. The Empress came rushing into the room, not to shush them, but to usher them quickly into his Majesty's sick room. He had heard the music and begged his mother to bring it to him.

The boisterous tone of the music quieted at the sight of the pale small boy. They all sat down while Takiko checked the pitch of each string, and then began softly to sing of springtime in the capital. The ladies wept a few homesick tears, but the Emperor's dark eyes were shining.

"Now the 'Dragon King,'" he ordered.

She sang the tale of the foolish jellyfish and the clever monkey for him and all his other favorites, ending with the lullabies with which she used to coax him into sleep. His head fell back upon the pillows, his face relaxed and happy. As his eyes began to droop, Lady Kiyomori signaled for the members of the court to leave the room, which they did silently and reluctantly.

At last only Takiko was left, barely plucking the strings and singing in a low croon. Empress Kenreimon'in tucked the quilts about the boy, and Lady Kiyomori extinguished the lamp. Takiko finished the song and then tiptoed away.

From that night on, there was a concert every evening in the Emperor's quarters. When Takiko began to play, there would be perhaps only the Empress, Lady Kiyomori, and the Emperor listening. But hearing the sound of the music, people would begin to gather from all over the house; indeed, someone would send word to the other houses of the compound, and before long, Takiko was playing for a large and appreciative audience.

General Munemori came to include himself among her admirers. He was not quite as fat now as he had been the year before, but his belly still fell over his sash and his eyes had a sleepy look about them. He smiled as he listened to the music, revealing teeth that were discolored and decaying. Takiko found him thoroughly repulsive and studiously avoided his eyes while she played.

One night after a concert, one of Munemori's retainers slipped a note into her hand, and Takiko looked up to see the general smiling significantly at her.

She fled to her quarters before daring to unfold it, and to her horror read a carefully penned poem, heavy with the general's perfume:

> *Upon my exile shines a crescent moon.*
> *Let me find comfort in its golden ray.*

"Mieko!" She shouted and the girl came running and knelt beside her. "What shall I do?" She threw the general's poem into the startled girl's lap.

"General Munemori?" Mieko asked with horror.

She nodded dumbly.

"But it's impossible."

"Oh, thank you, Mieko. I was sure you would think so, too. But what can I do?"

"He's old and fat. You're much too good for him."

"But he's the head of our clan."

"He's fat."

Takiko giggled. "But I cannot tell him that, can I? Let me see:

> *"The crescent moon looks down upon the fatted goose,*
> *And all her warmth turns cold."*

Mieko began to giggle, and then both girls were laughing until their sides hurt. "*Sh, sh,*" Mieko warned. "Someone will hear and you will be in trouble." She wiped the tears from her eyes. "We must be serious. He's likely to appear any minute without even a word from you, vain as he is." In strained whispers the girls debated what should be done. None of the court ladies were likely to have patience with a young upstart who thought herself too good for the attentions of their commander in chief.

"Lady Kiyomori."

"Do you dare? She's his mother."

In reply Takiko jumped to her feet and started out of the room. She did not want to say baldly that she dared approach Lady Kiyomori, but as a matter of truth, she did dare. Since that first night when Kiyomori's widow had held the little Emperor as any loving grandmother might, Takiko had had no fear of her. Respect, yes, great respect for her strength and courage and gentleness of spirit, but no fear. Lady Kiyomori had no fear of her son Munemori, of that Takiko was sure, and the wise woman would advise her as Fusa might if she were here. The thought of likening the grandmother of his Imperial Majesty to a peasant housekeeper seemed not at all incongruous. They were both wise and loving women. If Fusa were here, Takiko would go to her; since she was not . . . .

"Where are you going?" Takiko had not reckoned on the dour presence of Lady Chujo standing guard at her mistress's door.

"I must see Lady Kiyomori."

"At this hour? Madam has retired."

"It is urgent, Lady Chujo. I would not disturb her otherwise."

Mieko stood by, her eyes wide. She was afraid of Lady Kiyomori, yet she was even more afraid of this bead-counting attendant.

"You will not disturb her in any wise." Lady Chujo sniffed through her extraordinary nose. "What brazenness!"

Takiko could feel her anger rising. She put her hand on the sliding door. "I am willing for her Holiness to judge my behavior—and yours."

"You open that door, and I will call the guards."

Guards who would take her straight to General Munemori—the one person she was most anxious to avoid. Takiko looked at the lady's face in the dim lamplight. She was not bluffing; she would call the guards.

Mieko was pushing her elbow. "Show her the note," she whispered.

"What note?" Lady Chujo had the sharp ears of a true court lady.

"It is my own affair," Takiko replied testily, shaking Mieko's hand off her elbow.

"As you like." With a slight smile the lady began counting her prayer beads.

It was now Takiko who grasped Mieko's arm. "Come," she said. And to the lady, "I will tell Lady Kiyomori you threatened me."

"Indeed?" Her eyebrows went up, but she did not lose the rhythm of her prayer.

Once out of earshot, Mieko began to protest. "You should have shown her the note. At least you should have explained to her why you wanted to see Lady Kiyomori in the middle of the night."

Takiko let out a short peasant curse, a word which Mieko, protected child of the court, could not understand, though the feeling was unmistakable. "Do you think Big Nose would accept this note as an excuse? Don't be a fool, Mieko! Munemori is the chief of our clan. She's likely to consider me a traitor for refusing him.

She would probably collapse with joy if he sent her a poem like this."

"She would collapse with joy if any man sent her a poem." Mieko giggled. "They say her late husband died of fright the first time he saw her by sunlight."

"Be still, Mieko, I have to think." But Takiko was giggling, too. "I'll go to the garden. You go to my room and put some pillows in my bed. If anyone asks for me, tell them I'm sick—no, tell them—" She hit her forehead with the palm of her hand. "Mieko, what should you tell them?"

"Well, I might say that your horoscope forbids your entering any new alliances at this time."

"Oh, marvelous! He won't dare violate a taboo while under threat from Yoshitsune. But just in case passion is stronger than piety, I'll spend the night in the garden. Good night, Mieko."

"Good night, mistress." Mieko giggled despite herself. They both looked carefully up and down the hall, and then parted, quite pleased with their cleverness.

The garden behind the manor house was awash with moonlight. The steep hill at its rear hung like a subdued landscape on a painted scroll behind the soft arrangement of rocks and pine at its feet.

Takiko took a deep breath. Sea air mingled with the fresh perfume of the pines. The early autumn night was chill but alive, so unlike the musty odor of the house. She sighed with pleasure and settled herself behind a large rock at the end of the formal garden. If only she had her koto out here. It was a night for singing, with the Moon God nearly full above and a thousand stars dancing attendance.

There was a rustling among the pines. There was no wind. There must be an animal nearby. Indeed, deer had from time to time been discovered in the garden nibbling the precious herbs grown for medicine and seasoning. She studied the slope until she saw the place where the pines were being disturbed. Takiko was not afraid of animals. Goro had taught her that most were afraid of people, so she watched with curiosity to see what large animal—for a badger or weasel would hardly disturb the greens in such a way—could be making its way so boldly and quietly to the place of men.

For several moments the animal stayed perfectly still, as if watching the compound. At least, there was no movement among the pines, but Takiko kept her eyes fixed on the spot. She knew it was still there. She could almost feel its eyes. She shrank back into the shadow of the rock. She wasn't really afraid, but still . . . .

There was a tiny, almost imperceptible movement of the needles, and the moonlight caught a glint—something like a reflection from the face of a mirror. What animal would have a coat so bright, so metal-like that . . . ?

She gasped. There was only one animal who wore metal. She half rose. A guard must be summoned. But it had been her imagination. The branches were still, and nothing shone from under them. A piece of mica on the rock perhaps.

Then the movement began again. She watched, no longer calmly, but with her pulse racing and perspiration starting from her hot scalp. The creature was surely coming now down into the garden itself. She picked up a stone and waited.

She watched frozen as the man slipped the last few feet where the hill dropped off to the terrace and landed on his feet. Like a fox he slid behind another of the large ornamental rocks near the one that sheltered her. He was tall with a topknot, and she could see the shadow of his long sword by his side. He was not in armor. The metal she had seen must have been from his sword hilt, which even now caught the moonlight as he moved from rock to rock.

He was coming toward her. She lifted the stone above her head. She would try at least to stun him.

"Nightingale!"

He stood over her with his familiar lean face and long-remembered smell. She dropped the stone. "What are you doing here in the garden?" He asked it as though it were perfectly natural for him, a Genji samurai, to be in the garden of his enemies' stronghold.

There was no help for it now. She must scream and summon the guards. No matter that Munemori should find her in the garden or that Hideo . . . . Rushing down the mountain at Ichinotani like gods that terrible day. *He is my enemy.* A picture of her father's body . . . . She opened her mouth.

"No, no. I can't allow you to betray me." He pressed his large hand over her mouth. Despite everything, her body burned at his touch, but it was her mind responding angrily to her body's weakness that glittered in her eyes.

"They've made you into a Heike, have they?" His whisper was more exciting than the low voice she remembered. "What a shame. But it will all be over some-day, and then we can forget clan and Emperor and . . . ." He slid his free hand around her body. Merciful Kwan-non, must he torture her so?

"Can you tell me how many men are here on Ya-shima?"

She shook her head in a violent no.

He sighed. "Give me a few minutes. Let me get halfway up the hill. Then call anyone you like. All right?"

Her eyes flashed angrily, but she did not move her head.

"You do not want my death on your hands, and by the Gods I could not bear to take yours." He stroked her back as though she were an unhappy child. "I'll whistle." He dropped both hands and ran directly to the hill and began to climb. She stood like one turned to stone, watching the movement of the branches.

A gentle whistle came out of the darkness above. "*Hōhokikyo. Hōhokikyo.*" It was like the cry of a nightingale.

Takiko began to run for the house, screaming as she went, "Genji! Genji!" In a matter of moments guards were swarming into the garden.

Yes. She thought she had seen a Genji warrior.

How many?

Just one. She hung her head a bit.

Where did he go?

She wasn't sure. He had appeared from behind the rock, seen her, and disappeared.

With grumblings about moonstruck women, the guards spent the rest of the night combing the island for sign of the enemy. Scouts took a small boat and poled it over to the large island of Shikoku, but there was no sign of Genji anywhere.

Takiko did not even dare to tell Mieko what had really happened, and bore her humiliation silently. No one, including Munemori, believed she had seen a Genji warrior. But was not that just as well? She had done her duty as a Heike, had she not? She had been willing to betray the life of the man she loved for the safety of her clan and its Emperor. She had been willing. If they did not believe her, that was their fault. She had done her duty.

One result of the affair was that Munemori's admiration waned. His lieutenants would resent an entanglement with this hysterical girl. And on second thought a young woman so obviously a pet of his mother's might prove troublesome on other counts. At any rate, to Takiko's relief, he did not try to seek her out again.

TEN
The Rabbit Hole

Before the incident in the garden, Takiko had enjoyed her role as the darling of the court. Now the attention of the officers and the ladies shifted elsewhere. The Heike family had never been known for its intellectual prowess, but there arose a sudden interest in Chinese poetry, and one of Munemori's lieutenants who had made several trips to the Chinese court on trade missions for Lord Kiyomori became the center of cultural life on Yashima.

Takiko still played for the Emperor every day, but more often than not the audience numbered no more than four or five, including Empress Kenreimon'in and Lady Kiyomori, who rarely left the boy's side. The Emperor's younger brother was sometimes brought, though he was not the patient listener that his brother had always been.

Lady Chujo often came, but from the look she gave Takiko down the length of her nose there was no mistaking the reason. She was there simply because duty required her to attend Lady Kiyomori, not because she found the music pleasurable.

Takiko stared straight into the haughty face and tossed her shining hair. Why should she care for the fickleness of these dilettantes? What did they know of music or true beauty? Lady Chujo was only the worst of the lot with her beads and pretensions of piety.

Mieko remained loyal, and the two of them spent hours at the spring, attacking the manners and morals of their fellow courtiers. Sometimes they dug clay from the creek bank and tried to make vessels from it as they had done with the Emperor the year before. But now they did so half-heartedly, as both were aware that it was a childish exercise and that they no longer belonged to the games and amusements of childhood.

Mieko discovered men that fall, and would have fallen in love with a dozen young officers before the first frost, if Takiko had not kept a firm reign on her. It was not that she was jealous, or perhaps it was. How could she know? Mieko was her only friend and confidante. If Mieko really fell in love with one of these silly boys, what would happen to her?

Thoughts of Hideo were never far from her mind, and from time to time they would invade her consciousness like a legion of demons. Sometimes when she was playing for the Emperor, a single chord would recall the tone of his voice, and she would begin to weep, unable to control herself.

Her behavior was generally dismissed as part of her "hysterical" tendency. Was not she likely to see Genji warriors behind every rock? Only Mieko took her tears seriously and pressed her to share whatever was burdening her heart, but this Takiko dared not do. It was not that she did not trust Mieko; on the contrary, she trusted Mieko far more than she trusted herself. For although she never thought it out completely, she feared that once she admitted aloud her love for Hideo, she would have confessed herself a traitor, and she did not have the courage to face the possibility of this truth.

If she had been melancholy in the spring, it was nothing to the despair she felt now. The great orange persimmons became ripe, but she did not laugh with pleasure at their sweetness. She had vowed all year that she was languishing for one bite of an autumn pear, but when Mieko came running in one morning with the first ripe ones of the season, she was disappointed to see Takiko's lack of pleasure. Even when the girl bit into the crisp yellow fruit and the juice gushed out, running down her chin and into her lap, Takiko seemed only annoyed, not amused as she would have been the year before. What evil humors might possess her?

While Mieko feared for her friend's health, Takiko feared for her own sanity. She had heard of women driven mad by love, and she was sure that she was going to be one of them. For no apparent reason, she would be seized by fits of weeping. She plummeted into despair when a tooth of her comb broke. She lacked any interest in the sights and tastes that had once enticed and delighted her. While sitting quietly at the open doorway, his smell would suddenly come to her nostrils and she would be convinced that he was somewhere near. She would search the adjoining rooms and look in every cranny of the garden, retracing her steps a dozen times, her eyes bulging with anxiety and hope. Or she would hear, by chance, a bird call, and recognize in it his voice.

Or she would see out of the corner of her eye a tall male form and *know* it to be his, spinning about to meet one of the Heike warriors smiling in amusement at the peculiar girl she was so rapidly becoming.

She had never cared for the Gods or for prayer, but one bright November morning, so racked with fear and fruitless daydreams that she knew her reason would soon depart altogether, she climbed the hill behind the compound where she had seen him leave and tried to imagine that his feet had also stepped in just this place, that his hands had also grasped just this branch, that these same pine needles had brushed his body as he passed. Up and up she walked to the very summit of the hill, to the temple from the porch of which she could see far out across the sea, shining like burnished metal on whose polished surface some giant hand had dropped the islands. Their compound was on the south side of Yashima, its harbor sheltered by the much larger island of Shikoku, so that from the manor house no one could see the expanse of the Inland Sea. But now it lay stern and beautiful before her. It made her lonely to look down at it. Where could he be hiding? On one of those tiny islands out there? On Shikoku? Here on Yashima? Or had he set sail already for the mainland? Perhaps he was at this moment reporting to Yoshitsune all that he had discovered on Yashima. Her eyes left the silken tapestry of sea to look down on the fortifications facing it, fortifications never left unguarded against that day when ships flying white flags might be sighted, heading for Yashima. She shivered, and slipping off her clogs, slid quietly into the dark interior of the temple. In an adjoining room she could hear the monks chanting their morning prayers.

Princess Aoi had sent her to Kiyomizu Temple to

pray, and she had met him there—in a place very much like this. How young she had been then! She had been embarrassed when his hand touched her knee.

Takiko began to recite the sutras in defense against memories. She had brought no beads, so she held her palms together and touched her forehead to her finger-tips. She rubbed the tips together. The tips of her fingers on her left hand were callused from pressing down koto strings. She liked the feel of them. The roughness com-forted her. But she must pray. She had never memorized much of the scriptures. Goro had taught her love poems and proverbs when he should have been teaching her religion, so her memory soon faltered and she was obliged to repeat those few passages of the sacred writ-ings that she could recall.

Suddenly she knew. He was there. She hardly dared open her eyes for fear it would be another cruel illusion.

"How did you find me?"

She turned to look at him now. He was dressed as a monk, as he had been the first time she had seen him. "I—I wasn't looking for you. I came to pray."

He smiled his strong wide smile. "Then it is our destiny." He reached out and took her right hand from its position of prayer and stood, bringing her to her feet with him.

"How very beautiful you are."

She began to weep. She had thought she could not bear the dream, but the waking was even more over-whelming. She pulled her hand away and covered her face, falling again to her knees. Her body shook with the sobbing.

"*Sh-sh*"—he took her in his arms the way a father might take a child—"not here, not here." He picked her up and carried her through the rear entrance of the temple to a tiny hut at the back of the temple grounds.

He put her down and shoved open the low door. "This is my rabbit hole," he said, gently guiding her inside. There were no windows, and when he closed the door, she could see nothing of the bright morning outside. He lit an oil lamp which scarcely shed light beyond the tree stump on which it sat. The floor was of packed earth and felt cold through her cloth socks.

"My clogs. I left them on the temple porch."

His smile flashed white. "We'll get them. Don't worry." He spread a quilt across a pile of straw at one end of the hut. Once more he took her by the hand and led her the few steps across the room. "I have been longing for you since the first night at the house of Prince Kira when I heard you sing."

She could not reply but sat beside him on the quilt like an obedient child. She wanted to speak, but her mouth and throat were frozen. The chanting of the monks rose like the buzz of swarming bees. He raised her hair and ran a long finger across the back of her neck.

"So lovely," he said softly.

ELEVEN
A Visitor

The grasses blurred at her feet, and in her ears the chanting or buzzing or whatever it was rose to a deafening
crescendo and threatened to burst her skull. She focused
on her feet. Yes, she had on her clogs. Then on the sky.
It must be late afternoon. They were sure to have missed
her. Indeed, there was Mieko climbing up to meet her
from the garden.

"Where have you been? I've been crazy with worry."

"I had to pray."

Mieko looked at her with a puzzled smile, not knowing whether to believe her or not.

"There is a beautiful view from the temple, you
know."

"I'm sure there must be."

"Now I think I will bathe and change, so that I'll be ready to play for his Majesty a little earlier tonight." Her head began to clear.

"Yes, of course." Mieko did not move to obey, simply stared at her as though there was something in Takiko's face that she could not understand.

"I'm all right, Mieko." She could hear her own voice now inside her head, and it sounded like Empress Kenreimon'in. Did such an experience change one so much then?

"You'd better see to the water."

"Oh, yes, yes." The girl turned and ran to obey.

Takiko did not see him again that week, but Hideo saw her. He said so in the note he slipped under her koto as the traditional "next-morning" poem. His calligraphy was faultlessly masculine, and she read the thirty-one syllables over and over until they were indelibly stroked on her heart. What an astounding man—to creep into the very camp of his enemy to leave a love poem. Custom required this courtesy, but surely not at the risk of life! If she had loved him before, it was nothing to what she felt now. Love and pride lit her from within like a festival torch. She knew she was on fire but was as helpless to conceal it as she had been to stop her tears.

"Take care, little one," Lady Kiyomori said after Takiko had played for the Emperor one night. "Love is like a brushfire in August." But she had only stammered in reply. She did not care that everyone seemed to know that she loved, but she must never, never, betray his identity. Her own life was forfeit. She was traitor by the very nature of her choice, but his life—his life was more precious to her than eternal salvation. No one could ever know.

At the end of the week she found another note under her koto. She looked now every time she came into the room, hoping, fearing that he might try to reach her again. It gave directions to a fishing boat, anchored on the eastern beach. He would meet her there the following day at noon if she were willing. Willing? She could not imagine any demon of Hell who could keep her away.

And it was not a demon who kept her from the appointment, but a visitor who arrived that night on a small boat from the mainland.

She was playing for the Emperor when a maid came into the room and knelt quietly, obviously waiting for her to finish. The short hairs on the back of her neck bristled. She was afraid for him; Hideo was so rash. Surely he had not come boldly to the house to seek her.

But when she was dismissed, the maid approached her quietly with a strange expression on her face.

"You have a visitor, madam."

"Yes?" she said sharply.

"I directed him to the receiving room. He is waiting there."

Her heart was like the great cold bronze clapper of a bell banging against her chest as she followed the maid to the receiving room and slipped behind the screen.

Through the opaque screen she could see a small nearly child-sized figure. Not Hideo then. His height would have been unmistakable. "Yes? I am here."

"It has been a long time," the voice began.

Goro! She stammered a reply. "When? How?"

"I do not wish to cause you embarrassment by my coming so unexpectedly."

Did he know something? "No, no, you are welcome. I am just so overcome with surprise. I hope you come in good health."

"Yes, yes. I'm never ill. You know that."

"And my mother?"

"Well, she is well. Another child is due in the spring."

"And Ichiro?"

"Growing—spoiled. But so far he is healthy."

"And Fusa is well also?"

"Yes, yes. All are as well as could be expected."

"Then something is wrong?"

"I am a rude man, Takiko. You know that I've never learned the art of indirection."

"Then, what . . . ?"

"The Genji burned the house to the ground. All the crops were stolen, except those few we managed to hide in the ground. The peasants, any able-bodied men among them, have been conscripted. The women and children have fled to villages farther away in the mountains. Last month I sent Fusa back to her native village."

Takiko gasped. She tried to picture the scene in her mind. "But where do you live?"

"In the workshop. It burned poorly except for the thatching, and I've patched that."

"And I live here in luxury."

"We don't begrudge you that, Takiko. Believe me. I did not come to fetch you because we begrudge you this."

"Fetch me?"

"Your mother is with child. She wants you with her. Not only that, she fears for your safety here. Yoritomo will not leave Yashima in peace forever. Someday he will send Yoshitsune here. Should he prevail, there will be no mercy shown to Heike—man, woman, or child. Your mother cries every night for you and for what may become of you."

"But I—I cannot leave." She could not conceal the anguish in her voice. "My—my duty . . . ."

"Her Highness will surely release you—for your mother's sake."

"Oh, Goro, you ask too much!" When the words were out, she heard the sound of them and was frightened. "Father," she corrected herself. "Father, I play for his Majesty. He is ill, and the music cheers him. I'm needed here."

"Yes." His voice was quiet. "I know I place our humble needs against the needs of the Emperor. You were right not to address me as father. I have not come as your father to command you—but as poor Goro who loves your mother like a country fool and cannot bear to see her in pain." He rose to his feet. "The boat leaves at noon. Come with me, child. I beg you." He turned to go, then remembered something. "I fetched your koto. It is waiting for you."

She returned to her quarters in a fury of feeling. She would not leave, of course. That was impossible. She had her duty here. *Hideo, Hideo.* No, it was not just Hideo that kept her here. She could not be so selfish. She had a post of responsibility here as surely as any soldier of the Heike clan. If Goro and her mother could not see this, then she was sorry. But she would not leave Yashima. She left a note under her koto for Hideo. Perhaps he would come when she failed to meet him at the fishing boat. She prayed so as she made her way to the harbor to the tiny merchant ship bobbing in the surf. Goro came down the gangplank to meet her. His eyes looked first at her and then for some sign of porters with her baggage, but there was none. "So you are not coming?"

"No. My duty is here." She said it quite calmly and surely.

His eyes narrowed, and he tilted up his head in order to search her face. "You will break your mother's heart," he said and, turning abruptly, reboarded the ship without a backward glance.

How unfair he was! At least he could have waited long enough to let her send greetings to her family and Fusa. He was a cruel man—self-righteous and cruel. She had a boy take a basket of late pears on board and give it to him. Her mother should have some sign that she cared. Goro was likely to make her sound like some kind of unfeeling monster, when she *did* care for them. Under any other circumstances she would not have hesitated for a moment to go home, but now—now—she was needed here.

She ran all the way back to her quarters, but the note was still under the koto and remained there for three days until she herself tore it up and burned it.

TWELVE
Fire at Dawn

By New Year's she was convinced that Hideo had left the island. She could not be sure just when. So few ships other than Heike warships ever came to Yashima. It was possible that he might have left on the same merchant ship that Goro boarded, but the irony of that was too much for her, so she rejected the idea.

For a while she had waited for notes from him that never appeared; then she had searched for the fishing boat he had mentioned, but it was not at anchor where he had said it would be on that day. One morning at the end of the year, when the compound was in the flurry of New Year's preparations, she had made her way secretly to the "rabbit hole" behind the temple, but there was no sign of him there, not even a trace of his smell. She sat in the darkness and wept for a while, but, she said to herself, at least he was safe now. He was never safe on Yashima. The fact that he had gone should have indicated to her that something was stirring among the Genji. If he was no longer needed as a spy here—but the implications of his leaving were not clear to her. She only knew that he had gone, and she must clutch the hope that someday she would be with him again.

This was the substance of her New Year's prayers, but she did not forget to pray, however contradictorily, for the cause of her clan, the health of the Emperor, and the happiness of her family.

It was a long, cold winter. The women and children sat huddled in the drafty manor house and longed for spring. The little Emperor's cough, which had never really left him, returned in dreadful strength. Takiko played her koto and sang in the dark shuttered room, her mind as often as not far from the dismal sickroom, but the Empress and Lady Kiyomori still maintained that the music helped the boy, and she took some comfort that her refusal to return home was justified by their praise.

Word from the mainland was generally good. Yoritomo was installed in Kamakura, as jealous as ever, it would seem, of Yoshitsune's popularity and military genius. Since the battle of Ichinotani, he had kept his youngest brother closely in check and turned over the task of subduing the Heike to another brother, Noriyori, who was battling the Heike supporters along the southern coast with the vigor and success of a toothless man chewing ginkgo nuts. As long as Yoritomo feared Yoshitsune more than he feared the Heike, the Heike would be free to recruit and rebuild and prepare in earnest for their return to the mainland.

The plum blossoms bloomed and fell, and the smell of the first green pervaded even the corners of the musty manor house. The shutters were thrown open to the March sun. Spring was coming. Even Takiko felt it stirring within herself. She had been melancholy far too long. She would cast off the burden of lingering despair. Spring was hope. But the air was still cold, and even on the protected side of the island the March wind would blow with fury. Shutters were reluctantly closed against it, but everyone knew it would not be long until the cherry trees bloomed. Perhaps, before summer, they would be home.

But the wolf cub could not be kept forever in his den. Noriyori was getting nowhere, and Yoritomo was impatient for victory. Against all his better judgment he sent once more a commission to his youngest brother Yoshitsune. Bring back the Emperor. Bring back the Imperial Regalia.

With a yelp of delight, Yoshitsune and his pack raced to the seacoast. He rounded up a fleet of merchant vessels and one-time pirate ships. He was determined to set sail that very night before Heike spies could spot him, or his fickle brother could change his mind.

There was a gale blowing, but Yoshitsune was not enough of a sailor to fear the wind. Some ships were lost, to be sure, but those that arrived at the northeast tip of Shikoku made it in four hours rather than the usual two or three days. Yoshitsune was exultant. He led his thundering horsemen across the northern shore of Shikoku until they could look across and see the sheltered harbor of Yashima and the Imperial compound where the Heike slept. The true fortifications, as his spies had related, were on the other side of Yashima, facing the sea. It was almost too easy—like an unarmed merchant ship loaded with treasure, inviting plunder.

Takiko was awakened by a cry, and the sound of feet racing down the long wooden corridor. She sat up in the dark room not yet fully awake and tried to decipher the shouts. "Fires! Fires!" "The enemy . . . ." The rest was lost in the cacophony of cries and footsteps.

She jumped out from under her quilts. "Mieko, Mieko!" She shook the soundly sleeping girl. "There's some trouble. Wake up!" Mieko opened her eyes and smiled drowsily. "No, no. Something's wrong. You must get up!"

With this she ran to the door and slid it open. "What is it?" she shouted to a soldier rushing past her door.

"The enemy!" he yelled, never slowing. "At our rear. Shikoku."

This time she ran to the shutters facing the harbor and threw them open. It was not quite dawn, yet the sky seemed blazing with light. *But not from the east.* The light leaping into the still gray sky was from the south— from the shores of Shikoku. When she focused her still sleepy sight and powers on the scene, she saw what must have been a mile of bonfires just back from the coast. Soldiers had landed at the Heike rear. It was Yoshitsune, of course. And Hideo? Where was he? Oh, Hideo, Hideo, how was she to bear this day?

Lady Chujo came charging into the room, nostrils flared like a frightened war-horse. "Get dressed. We are surrounded. Munemori has given the order to take the Emperor and board a warship. We are helpless here. Helpless." Her voice was quavering, but she controlled it with a loud sniff and galloped off elsewhere to sound the alarm.

The two girls were wide awake now. They both dressed themselves. There was no time for rank or ceremony. Takiko ran the comb as quickly as she could through her own hair, ignoring several tangles. Both of them laid a change of clothing on a large silk kerchief and tied it up. Mieko hastily folded the bedclothes and put them away in the closet — even the enemy threat could not break this ingrained habit — and Takiko took the koto from the corner, wrapped it lovingly in a quilt, and hid it in the back of the closet. Once again she felt a keen pang of regret at leaving an instrument behind. Then they pushed the wooden shutters back into place and left the cheerless room for the madhouse of corridor and courtyard.

They were herded aboard the Imperial warship like a flock of chickens to the market. The soldiers were grim-faced and silent. Takiko's eyes kept focusing on the bonfires — there must be thousands of soldiers ashore behind those fires. She shivered and reached out for Mieko's free hand. They boarded the vessel together and obediently went into the familiar cabin and laid their clothing bundles down where Lady Chujo imperiously instructed them to. Some saint from the kitchens had sent on board rice cakes wrapped in seaweed. It seemed a humble breakfast for the Emperor's court, but no one considered complaining. They ate silently, and though Lady Chujo once broke the quiet to ask how any one of them dared have an appetite at such a time, everyone, including the lady herself, finished off his or her portion with gratitude. To eat was to pass the dreadful time in an ordinary way, and it comforted them.

Anchor was weighed. They felt the boat moving slowly off from shore. Takiko waited in vain for the feel of the sails catching the wind of the open sea. "We're stopping," she whispered to Mieko.

Indeed the order was given for the anchor to be dropped again. They couldn't be more than a few hundred feet from shore. "He's going to fight them here," she whispered again.

Mieko's eyes widened with fear. "Are you sure?"

"He would not stop here otherwise. There is plenty of wind if Munemori wants to escape them." She got to her knees. "Come on. Let's go on deck." Mieko looked at her wonderingly but began to follow, creeping on her knees toward the door.

"Where are you two going?"

"We would see the battle, madam, and give our men courage by our presence if we can." Takiko was on her feet now.

"Silly little fools, don't you know the danger? I forbid you to leave this cabin!" Lady Chujo blocked the small doorway with her body.

"Quiet, lady." It was Lady Kiyomori. "Perhaps the girl is right. Our men will be cheered by seeing that we have confidence in their victory today." She turned to the Emperor. "Your Majesty, do you feel strong enough to join me on the deck?"

"Oh yes, Ama." The boy's eyes were shining. And taking his grandmother's hand, he led his court out onto the deck of the warship. The Empress followed, carrying her younger son in her arms.

They were closer to shore than they had been at Ichinotani—just out of arrow range, Takiko guessed, though her only evidence for this was the fact that ships containing the archers were drawn about a hundred feet closer to shore than their ship. A single ship loaded with foot soldiers was making directly for shore where a long line of Genji horsemen waited.

"Yoshitsune!" Mieko breathed the awful name. It was unmistakably he at the center of the long line of horsemen, though no faces were recognizable at that distance. He wore white and purple armor under which sleeves and trousers of bright red silk emerged. His golden helmet had horns that rose more than a foot above his head. In his left hand, with the reins of his horse, he grasped his tall red and gold bow, his right hand waiting for the moment when he would draw his deadly sword. And now, rising in his stirrups, as though to still any possible doubt, he shouted and his words carried across the water: "I am Yoshitsune of the Genji, Imperial messenger, chief warrior of the Genji clan!"

As if in answer to a challenge, a foot soldier rapidly made his way through the shallow water, where the Heike warship had deposited him, and raised his arm toward the Genji line. Yoshitsune barked an order. A number of horsemen spurred forward. One of them galloped ahead of the rest, crying out his noble name in challenge to the Heike warrior.

The two men met with a clash of swords at the edge of the shallow water. The horseman might seem to have all the advantage, but the foot soldier's sword was a truer blade, and he shattered his opponent's weapon in the first clash. Confused, the horseman reined in his beast and tried to make for the safety of the shore, but the swift Heike soldier reached up and grasped him by the armor and began to pull him backward off his horse.

As they struggled, Yoshitsune himself galloped toward the scene. On board the nearest Heike warship the commander called for his best archer. An arrow was aimed at the heart under the purple and white armor.

But the archer, too, was spotted. With a scream piercing the blue morning sky, a Genji horseman spurred his horse like a madman and took between the plates of his armor and into his own body the arrow intended for his commander. He tumbled off his mount into the water.

Something like a sigh went up from both lines. For a few moments the only sound was the lapping of waves and the cry of gulls. The brave Heike soldier who had begun the duel returned to his ship grasping a bleeding shoulder. His comrades waited with respect as Yoshitsune ordered the bodies of his two dead retainers brought back to shore. The Genji line was reformed. In answer a battery of arrows from the Heike ship blackened the sky.

The battle was on in earnest now. Yoshitsune brought his troops into the water until the horses stood nearly knee-deep in the surf. Arrows from both sides hummed through the air with deadly accuracy, and above the hum were heard the cries of the victims and the revengeful screams of their companions.

Munemori waited fearfully for Yoshitsune to call up his reserves. The bonfires of their camp were still burning brightly. Why did the Genji chieftain taunt him so? From which direction would he strike next? How could he concentrate on the battle before him when he did not know which flank to protect? Yoshitsune must have ships somewhere, else he could not have come to Shikoku. Behind which island were they lurking?

Then an unbelievable thing—Yoshitsune's horse was swimming directly for the command ship on which Munemori stood. "What's happened?" the general cried.

"His bow—Yoshitsune's bow is in the water."

Munemori looked down. He could see the red and gold of the long bow bobbing on the waves below.

Yoshitsune was willing to die, it seemed, to retrieve it.
An archer raised his bow and took careful aim.

"No!" Munemori shouted. "He must be taken alive!
Get the rakes."

Munemori could not take it in. This demon who had
haunted and pursued him was coming like a salmon into
his net. He was almost in reach of the long rakes. Soldiers
leaned far over the balustrades to try to touch him. A
few tumbled in. But Yoshitsune proved an elusive fish.
Suddenly he caught hold of his bow and waved it in a
gesture of defiance, looking Munemori straight in the
face. Then with a cry to his horse he set the beast swimming like a dolphin for shore—or so it appeared to his
enemies.

The day wore on, and when still no reserves appeared, the women on the Emperor's ship began to relax
from their first terrors. The battle was going well. Had
they not all but captured the great Yoshitsune himself?
Only Takiko trembled as she searched the shore with its
Genji—alive and dead—and prayed for some super-
human vision to show her where *he* was. Though if she
knew and *then* saw him fall—it was all too terrible. She
turned from the scene with a shudder and went back to
where the little Emperor was seated on a barrel, fanning
himself more from nervous delight than from the heat.

"Isn't it exciting, Takiko?" he asked. She swallowed
and tried to smile. "Are we winning?"

"Of course, we are." Lady Chujo chose to answer to
the question. "Here, your Majesty. Let me have your
fan."

The boy obeyed as though he were her subject. The
lady gave the fan emblazoned with the red Imperial sun
to a sailor. "Take this and fasten it to the mast," she
commanded. "It will remind our enemies that they are

risking the wrath of the Gods today. They will find themselves opposing not only Heike but the Son of Heaven
himself."

The sailor hoisted himself up the tall mast and fas-
tened the fan, though not without further directions
from the tall lady below who wanted it placed on one
particular spot facing in exactly one direction.

But when the job was done, a cheer went up from all
aboard and traveled from Heike ship to ship as though a
flag of victory had been raised.

For a few moments there was silence from the shore;
then Yoshitsune summoned a man from the line and
pointed to the fan.

"We're out of arrow range, you arrogant fool!" Lady
Chujo snorted.

The horseman took an arrow from his quiver and
strung it on his bow. He took aim and held his position
for what seemed like eternity. Then *zing*—like a bee to
its hive the arrow arched over the long stretch of water—
and *thwack* pierced through the center of the rising sun
of the fan deep into the mast.

"A sign, O merciful Gods, a sign!" Lady Chujo
rushed into the cabin and slammed the door behind her.

On the shore a great shout went up. It was as though
the Genji with that one shot assumed that the victory
was now theirs.

Munemori gave the order. They must retire to Kyushu
at once before Yoshitsune called up his reserves and more
was lost than morale. And so they left Yashima and all
of Shikoku to the Genji. How were they to know that no
enemy camps lay about those campfires, that there were
no reserves, that Yoshitsune fought that day with a
hundred men against Munemori's thousands?

THIRTEEN
Plague

If it had not been for his wife's grief, Goro would have been nearly happy in his hut. Chieko had asked if she might do Fusa's work. She felt the need of work to keep her spirit occupied, and at night her exhausted body could fall quickly to sleep.

His little family would be close to contentment, Goro thought, had it not been for the girl. Chieko did not mention Takiko after his vain trip to Yashima, but sometimes coming home from the kiln, he would hear an awkward plucking of the koto, and when he entered the hut, he could see that her face was streaked from weeping.

When he tried to worry about the girl, he found he was only vexed by her stubbornness. And as he watched his wife's belly grow, he became more angry that Takiko was not here to help with the stooping and lifting and to chase after the lively Ichiro, who delighted in teasing his mother by dashing out of the house and hiding from her in the fields.

He did not want to send for Fusa. There was food enough for the three of them, but it was still only early spring, and there would be no crop until summer. What food they had must last until he could coax some return from his garden and paddy field. He put off sending for Fusa as long as he could, but by the middle of March it was evident that Chieko's time was near, and he could postpone it no longer.

Goro was out in the fields with Ichiro when he saw her coming from a long distance down the road. His first impression was that she was walking peculiarly, but he dismissed the thought. The road, usually rough, was even bumpier after the spring rains. Ichiro outraced him to throw himself into the arms of his beloved nurse.

When Goro reached them, his son was chattering joyfully and incoherently, his three-year-old vocabulary unequal to the feelings he was compelled to share.

Goro smiled over the boy's head to the woman. "You are more than welcome, as you must know," he said.

She bowed. "He has grown so much." When she lifted her head, there were tears in her eyes.

"You have come a long way. You must be tired."

She denied it, but he could tell it was only out of polite habit. They made their way to the hut where Chieko waited in the doorway. The two women bowed, and then laughing and weeping, they embraced, and Fusa was led inside more like an honored guest than an old servant.

Chieko had already prepared a meal of soup with a

tiny bit of their precious rice for each person, but Fusa refused to eat. They thought it was only out of politeness that she, remembering her real station, would not eat with them, but when they urged her, she replied with apparent sincerity that it was not custom that deterred her but weariness. Could they forgive her if she slept a bit? She was sure she would feel more like eating after a short nap.

Chieko laid a bed for her, and Goro took the boy well out into the fields where his noisy play could not disturb her. But he was deeply troubled. Fusa had never admitted to fatigue in all the years he had known her. The woman must be ill, really ill. He had been wrong to summon her, both for her sake and their own.

That evening Fusa forced herself up. She insisted on preparing the meager dinner, though again she herself took nothing beyond a few sips of tea. Afterward she let Ichiro sit on her lap and listened to his cheerful jumbled recital of the earthworm he had found and followed that afternoon and the beans that were sprouting in his father's garden.

She sang him to sleep with her store of country lullabies and carried his sturdy little body to his bed just as she had always done, but when she turned from him, even in the dim lamplight Goro could see that her face was drawn with exhaustion.

For two days she worked by sheer power of her will, but on the third day even this failed her. She could not rise from her quilts.

"You must send me away," she whispered to Goro hoarsely. "I am ill."

"How can we send you away when you are so sick? You can't walk a step, and we have no cart or ox."

"Then put me out of the house," she pleaded, "for the sake of the boy and yourselves." She stopped abruptly and turned her face to the wall. "Why did I come?" she moaned.

By night Fusa was burning with fever. They bathed her with wet rags, but her temperature rose all the higher. She began to rage. Her cries were for forgiveness. She had had a suspicion that the death in her father's village last week was not from a simple fever as some had said. There was a rumor. . . . She cried out in distress of body and spirit, and there was no comforting her. The boy huddled frightened in a corner of the hut.

"Shall we put her out as she asks?" Goro shouted over the delirious ravings.

"It is too late!" Chieko replied, and when he saw the papules erupting on the tormented old face, he knew she was right.

They burned the body and the precious bedding with it. They did so silently, never voicing their fears even to themselves. And when two weeks had past, Goro began to feel a little lightness despite himself. Perhaps they had escaped after all. Stranger things had happened. But that very night Ichiro cried out in his sleep, and when they went to him, his hand was covered with a bright red rash.

Chieko did not weep. She nursed him night and day. Goro told her she must rest, for her own sake and that of the child she carried, but she seemed never to hear his voice. She never left Ichiro's side until the day Goro took his once beautiful little body, now covered with running and dried-up sores, out into the field and burned it. She was too ill by then to accompany him. "Tell Takiko we saved the koto," she said once with such lucidity that it frightened him. But it served to focus his grief into a great anger. If the girl had come home—but she had refused. He would have killed her if he could.

By the time Chieko died, she was hideously disfigured. It was as though, monster that he was, everything beautiful he touched became ugly. He could not bear it. Instead of taking her body out to burn it, he set fire to the hut. He would destroy everything as he had been destroyed. He watched the flames begin to leap up. *"Tell Takiko. . . ."*

"To hell with Takiko!" he screamed and ran into the flames and pulled out the koto.

For three days he sat by the river and waited for the plague to take him, but fate, that cruel beast, would not give him even that little comfort. And when at last he saw that he was condemned to life, he gathered what he could from the ashes of the hut and threw together a crude shack over the ruins of the farmhouse. Although his bedding was gone, his wheel had not burned, so he turned himself to the molding of clay like a god starting creation all over again.

FOURTEEN
The Land of the Dragon King

Though Munemori was given to looking over his shoulder, only the wind was at their backs. No ships boasting the white flag of the Genji could be sighted. He dared then to stop along the southern coast of the mainland, where Heike sympathizers loaded his ships with provisions for the two-hundred-mile voyage westward to the Straits of Shiminoseki, where a Heike garrison at Hikoshima protected the narrow passageway between the tip of the mainland and the island of Kyushu. Tomomori, the commander of Heike forces at Hikoshima, knew these waters like the wrinkles on his face. Not even the arrogant Yoshitsune would dare engage the Heike in battle at sea. And as long as the Heike ruled the sea, the Genji could not triumph.

It was April. The southern sun beat warmly on the decks of the ship. The little Emperor spent every daylight hour basking in the warmth. His cough left him, and even on the meager diet of the long voyage his thin cheeks began to fill out.

"You are growing so big and strong," Takiko told him. "No one will recognize you when you get home."

He flushed with pleasure. "Sing me the song of the Dragon King," he begged.

"I can't do it well without my koto," she protested.

"I don't care. I can remember how it's supposed to go. Please . . . ."

She always obliged him, not because he was her Emperor, but because he was a little boy with so few of the pleasures of a child. It was all she could do to restrain herself from putting an arm around his thin shoulders and hugging him as she might have an ordinary boy like Ichiro. Ichiro, though, would never sit still long enough for her to sing him a song and would probably wriggle out of any embrace. She had never had much desire to embrace her brother when she was young, but she was a woman of fifteen now and often longed to hold in her arms someone small — or tall. She sang louder to quiet the visions that were forever lurking behind the simplest thought to catch her unaware.

" 'Oh, Mr. Monkey!' called the jellyfish. 'Come away with me under the sea to Dragon Land and feast on fresh melons and sleep in a silken bed.' "

For months the little Emperor had known all the words by heart, and he began to sing them now, a little shyly at first, but when she nodded and encouraged him, he sang louder in his piping soprano the dialogue between the silly jellyfish and the clever monkey.

They sang it to the end where the angry Dragon King

beat the jellyfish to a pulp and the Dragon Queen with no monkey liver to heal her illness says, "Then I'll just have to get well without it."

"And she did!" shouted the boy.

Someone was clapping, and they saw that it was his grandmother, Lady Kiyomori.

The boy ran to her. "Did you hear, Ama? I know all the words!" Then to Takiko, "I did, didn't I?"

"Oh, yes," she assured him. "Better than I do myself."

"Not better." He looked at her carefully. "You are teasing me."

"No, no. You quite surprised me. You know every word, and you have a splendid voice. When I get my koto back, we'll sing lots of duets."

"Do you hear that, Ama?" He was beaming.

The little nun put her arm around her grandson. "You'll be famous in history as the Emperor who was a great musician."

"Really?"

Both women smiled. "Of course," Takiko said. "His Majesty should have lessons when we return to court. Perhaps a zither."

"Or a flute," the boy suggested. "The flute makes beautiful music with a koto."

"Yes"—his grandmother hesitated—"when your lungs are strong, a flute."

Gulls circled over the ship and followed its wake. Sometimes a spring shower would send the more timid ladies scurrying for the cabin, but Takiko preferred to stand on the deck and hold her face up to the gentle rain. It was a quieting thing and more profitable than prayer for bringing peace to her inner struggles.

As they neared the straits, the ship sailed close to the

southern shore of the mainland, and the ladies amused themselves watching the land move past, pointing out shrines and farmhouses. Even animals could be seen and identified. So the day Takiko saw the fox, her first feeling was that of sheer delight. His coat shone red in the sun, and he raced along the shore at what seemed to be the same speed as the ship. Indeed, as the steersman detoured about some offshore rocks, the fox ran ahead, climbed a bluff overlooking the water, and turned back as if waiting for them, his lazy companions, to catch up.

"Isn't he marvelous?" Takiko cried as they came even with him. He seemed to be looking at her, his solemn burning eyes on her face.

"He's looking at you!" Lady Chujo grabbed her arm.

"I think he likes me." She felt proud to be singled out by such a majestic creature.

"Likes you?" The woman recoiled in horror.

A finger of ice struck Takiko's chest—a fox. The dead are known to seek out the bodies of foxes to house their naked spirits. She laughed shakily. "Lady Chujo would see an omen in every cloud and a ghost in every living thing." But she avoided the lady's sharp eyes as she spoke.

The fox turned and ran back into the woods. In a few moments Lady Chujo went into the cabin. They could hear her chanting her prayers, and silently Takiko prayed for the safety of all her loved ones, beginning as always with Hideo and ending with Goro, the thought of whom still had the power to irritate her. Dwelling on her irritation, she was almost able to forget her fears.

It was noon on a cloudless afternoon when they reached the narrow straits between Kyushu and the mainland. The steersman of the lead ship gave the signal, and all the warships dropped anchor well away from the shore. For in a few hours the tide would turn, and any lingering ships of the convoy would be furiously driven against the rocky shore of the mainland. Any man who sailed these seas knew that tide and granted it much respect. This gave Munemori an idea. Yoshitsune did not know the sea. When he came in pursuit, for he was sure to come, what if they came to meet him—here— where the riptide would drive his puny fleet onto the rocks? He could hardly wait for the next day when he would meet Tomomori at Hikoshima and reveal his plan.

Tomomori was not as enthusiastic about the scheme as Munemori had hoped. The risk was high, but then, who knew these waters as he did? He had sailed this sea in pursuit of pirates for many years, and the last few he had spent in these very straits. No man had lived more intimately with the tides than he. Yoshitsune was a great general—no man who was not a fool would dispute that—but he did not know the Inland Sea, nor did any of his commanders.

It was the twenty-fourth of April, 1185, when word came that a fleet of ships flying the white flag of the Genji had been sighted. It was not a puny fleet. Yoshitsune had gathered to himself several hundred ships, many of which could be seen flying the emblems of Shikoku clans which Munemori had presumed were loyal to the Heike.

But he did not let anger at these betrayals muddle his strategy. At Tomomori's suggestion the large Chinese warships at their disposal would be manned by the weakest troops. The enemy, thinking the commanders and the Imperial court were on these larger vessels, would attack them first, only to be surrounded by the ordinary warships bearing the braver and more powerful warriors of the Heike forces.

With this maneuver they would engage the rattled

Genji convoy until early afternoon, then quickly with-draw to Hikoshima and let the riptide finish their task.

Nothing is so blue as an April sky over the Inland Sea. And that morning some god dipping down from the heavens would have seen it as a beautiful sight, the two great fleets moving toward each other in the narrow straits, against a background of white-capped waves, and rugged rock jutting out of the water with twisted pines clinging to its treacherous face. The ships were colorfully caparisoned for war with rich draperies and emblems of the families they bore. On the foremost mast, the ships traveling west bore the white flag of the Genji, and those sailing boldly eastward into the straits to meet them flew the blood-red flag of the Heike.

The Emperor and his court were allowed to sit quietly under the shade of a drapery, but they were warned by Munemori not to move to the edges of the deck or to call attention to themselves—this last being pointedly directed at Lady Chujo. The fan incident was never referred to explicitly, but no one had forgotten it. This ship would be kept at the perimeter of the fighting, but not so far out of line that the enemy would become suspicious of the importance of its passengers. If the ship were attacked, the Emperor with all the women and children aboard was to retire immediately to the cabin and to wait there for further instructions.

As soon as the two sides engaged forces, it seemed evident that the Heike ruse was working. Yoshitsune's ships sailed quickly to the sides of the great Chinese war-ships and hailed arrows upon their decks. Munemori gave the signal, and the lesser ships slowly began to sail into a nooselike formation around the heart of the battle.

The invincible Yoshitsune had fallen for their trick. His men were boarding the Chinese vessels now, cutting paths of blood across the broad wooden decks, but from behind, the Heike arrows descended with the deadly aim of falcons upon their prey.

Munemori could not disguise his satisfaction. Who could despise him now? Had he not outwitted the fox of warriors, the great Yoshitsune himself? And in four hours the tide would turn.

Suddenly a great shout rose from the deck of Yoshitsune's vessel. "What is it?" Munemori cried to the forward watch, and the question was called out from ship to ship, and then the reply returned.

"The small white cloud above the warship, sir. Yoshitsune has proclaimed it a sign from Heaven. Hachiman, the God of War, flies the white flag of the Genji — so he says." The explanation began to falter under the Heike commander's black look.

"A monstrous lie."

"Yes, my lord."

But the cries of courage and the renewed vigor of the Genji forces were apparent to Munemori, and although his own men still held the advantage, he was no longer swaggering upon the deck of his ship. Where was *his* sign from Heaven? Was he not the protector of the Emperor and guardian of the three Imperial treasures? He was a man of the sea, and it was to the sea that he looked for a sign. It was then that he saw the dolphins, a great school of them, more than he had ever before seen at one time in these waters.

He called a diviner to his side. "What do those dolphins signify?" he asked.

"Dolphins are a sign of good fortune, my lord," replied the seer.

"Yes, yes, I know. But whose good fortune? Mine or Yoshitsune's?"

For a moment the diviner kept his eyes on his toes. "If"—he hesitated—"if they turn back from our ships, the enemy will be destroyed."

"And if they do not?"

The man whispered something which in the noise of fighting Munemori could not hear.

"And if they do not?" he again demanded.

The man raised his voice so that it was barely audible. "If they come to us, then we—we are in danger."

Munemori turned abruptly from the diviner and fixed his eyes on the school of dolphins in the fascination of terror. They came straight for his ship. Turn! Turn! he willed. Turn! But the dolphins would not be turned. The whole school came to the side of the command vessel, leaped into the air, and then dived under the ship and passed out of sight.

His eyes bulging with strain and his throat dry, Munemori turned his attention once more to the battle. The Genji attack was ferocious, but his men were holding their own. He glanced at the sky. Time must not become their enemy as well. He cleared his parched throat and gave a cry, "*Eiiii!* Death to the traitors!" His cry was echoed from Heike to Heike, and they began to beat back the foe.

It was time to re-form, if they were going to take advantage of the tide. Tomomori ordered the Heike ships back. The Genji had already boarded a number of the Chinese warships and were engaged in man-to-man combat upon the decks. These ships could not comply, but the rest pulled back and made a new formation.

"Warships!" The cry went up from both sides as a fleet of vessels was sighted approaching from the open seas to the east.

"What color flag do they fly?" Munemori asked his lookout.

"No flag, sir, an emblem. But I cannot make it out."

The Genji lookout being farther to the east deciphered the emblem first and passed the word, so that the shout was heard before long even on the Heike side.

"It is the emblem of the High Priest of Kumano." Munemori gave a sigh of joy. His Holiness bore a great debt of honor to the Heike from the time of his father Kiyomori. What should he care for dolphins when the High Priest came with two hundred ships loaded with warriors? There was no need to worry about the tide. With these reinforcements, they could finish the enemy off before the tide grew too swift. He ordered his fleet forward into the narrows.

The sacred convoy advanced toward the scene of battle. The flight of arrows was halted as both sides, Genji and Heike, did obeisance. But then, unlike the dolphins, the warships turned and, hoisting a white flag, joined the Genji convoy.

"May you be cursed by your own God," Munemori muttered as he watched the High Priest's ships join the line of his enemy, for now he found himself fighting for the very existence of his clan. They must get out of the narrows and retreat to Kyushu. He called the order to the lookout to be passed from ship to ship. The steersman began his turn, but as he did so, an arrow sang across the deck striking him between his armor plates and sending him to the boards flapping like a wounded quail. The ship lurched.

Munemori shouted for someone to seize the rudder, and a terrified foot soldier did so, but he had never steered a boat before. It began to spin; the sails flapped ominously. At last a sailor who had at least some notion of how to hold a rudder made his way through the confusion of the deck to snatch the rudder and steady the ship.

"The steersmen!" shouted the lookout. "They are aiming only for the steersmen!" And when Munemori looked, he saw to his horror ship after ship going into wild spins, and under him he could feel the speed of the tide quickening.

"Sir." An aide touched Munemori's elbow. "Lord Shigeyoshi goes to the enemy." Munemori followed the outstretched arm of his lieutenant. The ships bearing the emblems of Shigeyoshi of Shikoku had indeed struck their red flags and were making deliberate speed toward the Genji convoy.

Meanwhile Tomomori, Munemori's second in command, ordered a small boat put into the water. The oarsman directed it back toward the vessel carrying the Emperor. There was no need to row; the tide sped them to the ship's side.

Tomomori half rose, steadying himself on the shoulder of his aide. "You see what we have come to!" he shouted. "Clean up the ship and throw all garbage and filth into the sea!" A rope ladder was swung over, and the commander scrambled up onto the deck. The court watched as though stunned as the general rushed about the deck, sweeping dust from the corners with his own hands, throwing overboard anything he found not tied into position.

"How does the battle go?" Lady Kiyomori's quiet voice asked the dreaded question.

"Oh"—Tomomori turned from his cleaning—"you ladies will soon be entertaining some handsome knights from the east!" Then he sat down on the deck with a great burst of raucous laughter.

"How can you joke at a time like this?" Lady Chujo shouted. For a moment Takiko feared she might jump upon the general's body like an enraged tiger. But Tomomori sobered.

"Prepare yourselves, your Highnesses." He bowed toward the Emperor and his mother, Empress Kenreimon'in. "It cannot be much longer." He bowed again and, without raising his face, scrambled over the deck into his small boat.

The Heike ships were no longer manned by steersmen who knew this tide. Yoshitsune's were, and they pushed the Heike fleet nearer and nearer the rocky shore of the mainland. More Heike ships lowered their red flags and saluted the Genji convoy. Like the sound of a thunderclap, the lead warship struck the rocks and splintered like an ill-made toy.

Meanwhile three Genji warships had drawn so close to the Emperor's ship that Takiko fancied she could make out the embroidery patterns on the warrior's sleeves. Takiko and Mieko sat trembling together upon the deck. *It will soon be all over*, Takiko thought, though her mind was too paralyzed to imagine what "all over" might mean to any of them.

She saw Lady Kiyomori rise abruptly and enter the cabin. For a moment Takiko wondered if this was the signal for all of them to take refuge there as they had been directed that morning, though no one had given an order. It was impossible that only this morning she had been singing of the Dragon King with that pale boy.

But Lady Kiyomori did not linger inside. She was soon back on deck, dressed in a gown of dark gray mourning. In her sash she had bound a long sword, and in her hand she carried a carved wooden box like a jewel casket. This she put down as she tucked the long skirts of her gown into her sash. She put the casket under one arm, and with the other she drew the boy Emperor to her side.

Had she gone crazy like Lord Tomomori? What was happening? Takiko got to her feet and would have gone toward the little nun, but seeing peace in the dark eyes, she hesitated.

At that moment Lady Kiyomori spoke. "I am only a woman," she said quietly, "but I will not fall into the hands of our enemies. As I have always in the past, I will accompany our Sovereign Lord Antoku." Her clear gaze swept the faces of the court. "Let those of you who have the will, follow me." She moved, the child at her side, to the gunwale where she took him up in her arms.

The boy lifted his anxious face as though searching for his mother. His grandmother carried him a step forward. "Where are you taking me, Ama?" His pale face turned fearfully to her serene one.

"Our once lovely land has become only a valley of misery and destruction. There is a land beneath the waves of pure happiness, another capital where no sorrow dwells. It is there that I am taking my Sovereign."

She turned first to the east and bade farewell to the God of Ise, and then to the west with a prayer for the mercy of the great Buddha. Then in a moment she was over the railing and into the sea, taking with her the Emperor and two of the Royal treasures.

To Takiko it was as though someone had come and ripped out her vital organs. Like a disembodied spirit, she watched the scene about her. Empress Kenreimon'in was the next to move forward. She picked up her younger son and followed her mother's path with slow deliberate steps. But someone rushed forward and was ahead of her at the railing.

The great ugly face was flushed a deep red, and the huge comic nose, even redder than its setting, appeared more grotesque than ever. "I go!" Lady Chujo cried out in her rasping voice. "Bear witness all of you that at the last I committed my spirit to Amida Buddha and died without fear!" She leaped overboard and landed with a splash on the water, her layers of kimono billowing out and keeping her bobbing on the surface, but only for a short time. They could hear her chants as the heavy garments soaked up the sea and dragged her to its depths.

Empress Kenreimon'in went next, dry-eyed and with little ceremony. "Farewell, my friends. I thank you all." She tightened her arms around her younger son and disappeared over the railing.

Others followed, some with speeches, others softly with prayers. Takiko felt someone touch her sleeve. "Do you go, my lady?" Mieko whispered.

"I—I." Her throat closed, and she found she could not answer.

"You will forgive my rudeness," Mieko murmured humbly, "if I precede you." She moved gracefully around her mistress and joined the line at the gunwale.

No, Mieko, Takiko pleaded silently. *Don't desert me.* But Mieko did not look back. She tucked up her robes and jumped without a word. Takiko covered her face with a groan.

She would have gone then. She often said to herself later that at the moment Mieko jumped, she herself had been given the courage to follow. But she never knew truly what she would have done, for at that moment Genji soldiers boarded the ship and she was bound and passed across the railings to the deck of a Genji warship.

FIFTEEN
The Ill-Made Cup

Takiko lay bound upon the deck. She might have lain there for several hours or only for minutes. She would never know, so numb was she to any sensation of life or time. But at length a soldier carried her into a small cabin on the Genji ship and deposited her against the wall like a sack of rice. He yanked loose her bonds and slammed the door.

After the brilliance of the April afternoon, it took her a few moments to adjust to the dim light, but she was immediately aware of the presence of others in the room. She was recognized before she could see the speaker distinctly.

"So, little Takiko, you are saved as well."

She did not recognize the voice at once, though later she realized it must have come from one of the ladies who had been in the cart on their first flight from the capital. She seemed to have no voice to reply but sat in the semidarkness, trying to decipher the faces of her fellow prisoners.

Was anyone she cared for among them? Mieko? Lady Kiyomori? The little Emperor? But how could she face any of them? She closed her eyes and let her head droop forward wearily.

The door slid open. "On your feet. All of you. Now that we are out of the tide the general demands a counting of the prisoners."

Takiko, being nearest the door, was first upon the deck, and thus could see each lady of the Heike court as she emerged from the dark doorway. Each shivered as she came out into the breeze, for their garments were soaked:

Lady Midori, whose voice she had recognized; Lady Chuba, another of Empress Kenreimon'in's attendants; Lady Kate, who had been keeper of the Empress's wardrobe, with two of the young servant girls who had assisted her. Then, blinking in the bright sunlight, Empress Kenreimon'in in her gorgeous robes dark and heavy with water, her beautiful hair plastered against her face. She held her younger son tight against her wet garments. The child clung to his mother in terror, but the Empress's back was straight and her head erect.

And that was all. Takiko waited, praying, but no one else emerged. Not Lady Kiyomori with her shaved nun's head, nor the pale little boy Emperor she had taken with her. Not Mieko. How could she bear this? Not Lady Chujo, so ugly, so grotesque, even in the valiant act of death.

"Your name?" The soldier had evidently asked before and was repeating the question with annoyance.

"Takiko," the girl whispered.

"Speak up!"

She raised her head. "Takiko."

A scribe took down her words. "Your father?"

"Lord Moriyuki of the Heike," she whispered.

"Who?" bellowed the impatient man.

"Goro!" she cried. "Goro, the potter of Shiga."

The soldier gave her a look that she took to be a sneer and moved on to question the next in line. Takiko turned toward the sea. The ship was safely out of the tidal current, anchored not far offshore from Kyushu in a sheltered cove. On the far shore the wreckage of what had been the Heike fleet cluttered the rocky coast. On a nearby ship she could see other prisoners being questioned. So there was hope—some hope—that more had been saved. If only Mieko and the boy—Lady Kiyomori was nearly a saint; she would not mind dying quite so much.

No one brought fresh garments for the Empress or any of her attendants. Indeed, the guard snorted when Lady Midori suggested it. "Then let us at least retire, so that we can take off the upper layers of our robes and spread them out in the sun to dry," the lady pleaded. This was to be allowed, so all those with wet garments, all the prisoners that is except Takiko, went inside the cabin to disrobe. She started to follow them, but suddenly, more ashamed than ever of her dry garments, remained where she was, pretending to study the destruction on the opposite shore.

"I feared to find you dead, or at the very least looking like a drowned rabbit, and here I find you more beautiful than ever."

She was afraid to turn around—and ashamed. He must know what had kept her from leaping over that railing with those she worshiped and loved.

"I can hardly believe my fortune." He did not touch her, but his voice stroked the place within where all her hurts were stored. She began to shake with the tears she had not shed.

"*Sh, sh*," he said, though she was not making any sound. "I cannot be seen here talking too long. But listen to me. Many who have survived today will die yet, and others, if Yoshitsune is merciful, will be permitted to enter the convent. But you"—he gently touched her hair. "But we cannot have you shaved and imprisoned behind a convent wall. Say nothing to anyone, but when we get to the capital, watch for me. I will have you free, or . . . ."

She turned toward him now and was dazzled by his beauty. His yellow silk sleeves were embroidered with tiny lavender iris, and the plates of his armor were red and deep purple. He had taken off his horned helmet and was holding it in the crook of his left arm. His face was deeply tanned. Their eyes met, and though he did not touch her, she could feel the embrace of his look. It was more than she could bear. She closed her eyes.

"I must go," he whispered. She nodded dumbly and tried to speak. "Bear yourself carefully," the words were in her throat, and her lips moved, but no sound came out. He had not waited for them at any rate. He was already at the rail and over, climbing down the ladder into a small boat below.

After a year and a half in exile, the Heike were going home. The songs they had sung and the dreams they had shared about this return seemed full of bitter irony now. For they were not returning in triumph to restore their young Emperor with his three Imperial treasures to his rightful place once more. They were coming, were being brought rather, like the useless hulls of harvested grain, which even if burned provide only a puny warmth.

And the Imperial treasures? The chest containing the sacred mirror had evidently proved too heavy for Lady Kiyomori, so the Genji had rescued it from the cabin just before the ship was abandoned to crash into the rocks.

The wooden case containing the sacred jewel was discovered several hours later floating on the waves. But the sword—Yoshitsune sent diver after diver into the depths the next morning, but it was never found. Nor were the bodies of his Imperial Majesty and his grandmother recovered. Kiyomori would have been proud of his little wife, who had proved in the end more of a trial to his enemies than his warrior sons.

Within a few days, the survivors on the ship bearing Empress Kenreimon'in's party were aware of what Heike survivors the other ships of the fleet were carrying to the capital. Munemori had been taken alive. The Empress had no particular affection for her brother, but she grieved that his death could not have been honorably accomplished in battle. What fate Yoritomo might envision for him was too horrible to contemplate. The Genji chieftain would never remember, the Empress knew, that after the last wars Munemori's father had spared Yoritomo's life and that of his brothers. Men did not remember the acts of mercy of their enemies. They only remembered obligations for vengeance.

The Empress was a far gentler woman than her mother, but she had inherited at least as much of Kiyomori's raw courage as her brother. So she did not give herself over to mourning for her dead son and mother but busied herself comforting her living child and the ladies aboard, who in their fears and confusion seemed to her like other children who must be tended and fed. As for her own life, she cared little. She considered that she had drowned in the straits and had no further cause for anxiety about her fate. There was nothing more that they could do to her.

She was especially gentle with Takiko. By her own manner she forbade any mention to be made of the fact that the girl had been taken on the deck rather than out of the water. She herself broke the news that Mieko's body had been found and held Takiko in her arms while the girl sobbed, the tears finally bursting the cask where the shame and anguish of all these terrible days and weeks had been tightly squeezed.

The Empress was only a little younger than Takiko's own mother, and the young Prince was about Ichiro's age; and as they neared the capital, Takiko began to hope that Hideo could keep his promise, that she could be set free and go home, O impossible dream, that some-day she could . . . . But to dream thus when those about her faced the annihilation of every dream seemed like further evidence of her traitorous nature. So she com-manded her daydreams to cease, though she had no such power over her dreams at night, nor did she really desire it.

It was dusk when their ship docked at Rokuhara—or at what remained of Kiyomori's once great estate. The word had spread that the victorious Yoshitsune with his Heike prisoners had arrived, and great crowds had come out from the capital to cheer the victors and scream con-tempt upon the defeated. The mob gathered about the gangplank, and though the Genji guardsmen made valiant attempts to keep them back, they shoved forward to stare or spit as their natures demanded.

Takiko followed the Empress, who held her son's hand and kept her head high. No one quite dared to spit on her, but when Takiko, of whom they had no knowledge, disembarked, they rushed forward as though to pay in double what they had hesitated to inflict upon her Majesty.

Takiko shrank back in terror from their twisted faces. Torches had been lit against the growing darkness, and the flickering light made the surge of the mob appear like that of ghostly dancers in a fantastic nightmare. She closed her eyes. Someone grabbed her roughly, and she could feel herself half lifted and half pushed away from the line of prisoners. She opened her mouth to cry out, but a large hand was clapped over it.

She opened her eyes wide to see what was happening to her. Even in the near darkness she could make out his face. He shoved a kerchief-wrapped bundle into her arms. "Clothes," he said hoarsely into her ear. "Change quickly and go home."

"Home?" she echoed.

"To Shiga—to your father's house." His voice softened. "I'll come to fetch you"—he grasped her arm in an iron grip—"as soon as I can." He turned abruptly and shoved his way back toward the line of prisoners and soldiers in the center of the mob.

She watched him go until suddenly aware of how conspicuous she must be in court robes, she clawed her way to the edge of the crowd. She would never have escaped except for the darkness and the mad tenor of those about her who were competing so fiercely to insult the captives that they hardly turned when she forced her way through their midst.

She headed for the merchant stalls perched on the river bank and slipped behind one of them into the darkness. Her feverish fingers tugged frantically at the knot in the kerchief, then gave up and began to loosen the sash of her robe. By the time she was down to her final court garment, her body was shaking less drastically, and she could kneel and concentrate on the stubborn knot.

"What is it, dearie? Have you lost something?" A bent figure slid out of the darkness from the side of the stall.

Motionless, Takiko watched the shadow move toward her. She had no lie, no possible lie to offer, so she waited, the perspiration soaking her thin remaining garment.

"One of those painted ladies from Sixth Avenue, are you?" The old woman had thrust her face right into Takiko's. Her breath was fetid. "A little out of your territory, aren't you, my pretty one."

"Cruel to me," she managed to stammer. "Everyone left to go to the docks, so I. . . ." She fumbled frantically at the knot, and it gave at last.

The woman grabbed her hair. "If I take you back, they'll have a pretty reward for me." Takiko struggled to pull loose, but the woman's grip, strong with greed, was not to be broken.

"Look, Auntie," she said, altering her voice to a wheedling tone. "My lovely silk garments, I have no more need of them. Let me go, and you may have them." The old head cocked in disbelief. "All of them." Then as proof of her sincerity, she began to slip out of the remaining garment. The old woman released her hold on the hair near Takiko's scalp, but kept a firm hand on a large hank farther down, as though keeping a prize monkey on a chain.

It did not make the change of garments easy, but it made it possible, and Takiko pulled on the peasant trousers and blouse, slipped her feet into straw sandals, and tied the rough sash about her waist. A narrow band remained.

"If I am to tie up my hair," she said quietly, "you'll have to release me, Auntie." The old woman did not comply, but pulling her along, stooped down and picked up the thirteen garments and sashes strewn on the ground. She dropped them on the kerchief.

"Tie them up," she ordered.

Takiko dropped gingerly to her knees, but the old woman had lowered her arm so there was no fear of further yanking. And there in the darkness, except for the leash of hair, Takiko might have been the Empress's lady of the wardrobe as she carefully folded each garment and stacked them upon the spread kerchief. It was her captor's turn to be anxious.

"Hurry up," she demanded.

Takiko quickly and deftly tied up the kerchief and handed it to her. In one swift motion the old woman released the girl's hair, grabbed the parcel, and scuttered away out of sight.

Her first trial past, Takiko bound up her hair with the band Hideo had provided. Alas, it was far too long. How could she pass for a peasant boy with hair like this? Had she scissors she might have cut it on the spot, but since there were none, she tucked the long tail down into the back of her blouse, where it tickled her back but at least was not so conspicuous.

And now, what? Must she start out for Shiga tonight? It was a full day's journey by ox cart to Goro's farm. Could she make it, alone and on foot, at night without food or weapons? But how could she risk entering the city? And who would help her? Her aunt, Lady Uchinaka? Princess Aoi? Could she risk presenting herself at their gates? What sort of new loyalties might these noblewomen have sworn in the years since they had been her protectors? And even if the women themselves did not betray her, there was a host of greedy servants to be reckoned with.

She only knew one other person in the capital — Kamaji, the merchant whose recommendation had brought her to the capital from Goro's farm more than two years before. Perhaps out of obligation or out of friendship for Goro, he would aid her. All the same, as she made her way across Gojo Bridge still crowded with those who had come to see the sights, she wished she had been able to preserve one silk kimono to offer the merchant.

She played the part of country bumpkin as best she could, drawing on her memories of Fusa's nephews who wiped their noses on their sleeves and spoke in guttural bursts of one-syllable words. At first everyone she asked seemed as stupid as the part she played, but at last she met someone who had heard of Kamaji and had some vague notion of where his shop was. She was forced to bear another false direction or two, but by the time the moon was high, she had found the merchant's sign. His shutters were closed and locked against the night. She could not bring herself to bang upon them at this hour and risk the man's wrath, so she curled up in a nearby alleyway and waited through the cold night, not daring to sleep.

At last dawn came, and with it the sound of shutters rumbling open before shops up and down the street. A servant boy came out of Kamaji's shop and began to sweep the street before it.

She got up, stretching her sore body, and went to the front of the shop. "Excuse me," she whispered to the servant boy. "I have a message for your master."

He looked at her oddly, and she realized too late that she had forgotten her country speech. But the boy made no remark, simply turned. She followed him inside and waited beside the doorway for the merchant to appear from the back of the shop.

The boy hung about curiously, but Takiko bowed to the merchant and then stared at the boy. He blushed and left to continue his sweeping.

"What's your business, boy?"

Takiko went down on her knees this time and bowed her body on the earthen floor of the shop. "Forgive me, Kamaji. I did not know where else to turn."

"Who are you?"

"Takiko, sir. Perhaps you remember. I am Goro's daughter that you . . . ."

"The pretty one?" He leaned down. "Get up, child." She stood but kept her eyes downcast. She did not want him to think she presumed on his kindness.

He was quiet for a moment, as though waiting for some explanation, but when there was none, he cleared his throat and said a little more loudly, "Well, suppose you eat breakfast with me."

Takiko dared look him in the face. "I must tell you, sir. . . ."

"Must? Nonsense. If I know nothing, I can be accused of nothing, right?"

She nodded gratefully.

"I can make arrangements for you to get home today, and then you're Goro's problem—though I might enjoy prolonging such a pretty problem for a few days." But he said it not in a lecherous way but as any merchant evaluating a prospective purchase.

After breakfast he sent his boy to the bridge area to

the home of a fellow merchant who was planning a trip to the towns near Lake Biwa. The girl could travel most of the way with this caravan, which would provide some safety along the road. Since the troubles began, many formerly honest men had been driven to thievery, and with competition so fierce, those bandits who preyed upon travelers were more desperate than ever.

Kamaji had food packed for her, and they sat on stools in the shop waiting for word that the caravan was ready to leave when, at last, she summoned the courage to ask, "Have you any news of my family?"

"Not since the fall," he said. "Goro came in himself, the first time, you know. He brought me those—" He waved his hand toward a shelf of pottery. "He said it was on his way, but he didn't say where he was going."

So she had seen Goro since the merchant had. But she gave no indication of this. "And my mother was well then?"

"So he said." He leaned toward her. "The house was destroyed, but he said they had enough to eat. You mustn't worry."

"No," she said, and got up and went to the shelf. It held a rather typical variety of Goro's work, except for one teacup in the Chinese style. She had never seen such a misshapen vessel. Goro despised absolute symmetry, she knew. But this strange cup looked as though the potter had tried to wring it like a piece of laundry. Even the lid was a grotesque fit. And the brilliant black glaze had been smeared on haphazardly so that the grays and yellows of the original clay broke through. What had Goro been thinking of? And why should Kamaji place this joke against pottery on the shelf among all the loveliest of his pieces?

She picked up the cup and turned it over. Yes, there

was Goro's sign dug into the bottom. He had made this thing. She lifted the lid and gasped. The underside of the lid had been painstakingly gold-leafed. Etched in the gold was a delicate line painting of a bird in flight—perhaps a nightingale. Reverently she replaced the lid and put the cup in place.

"Strange little man, isn't he?" Kamaji said gently.

Anger flared inside her, but she suppressed it and smiled at him. He meant no disrespect.

"Are you still playing the koto?"

"Not lately," she said softly, coming back to where the merchant was seated.

"No, I suppose not," he said and let the matter drop.

It was nearly noon the next day when the caravan reached the fork of the road where it would continue eastward toward Lake Biwa and she must turn southeast toward the river. The merchant had estimated that the remainder of the trip should take three or four hours if she kept a brisk pace, and since he presumed her to be a farm lad (though her hands were curiously delicate), he had assured her that she could be at Goro's estate by midafternoon.

Takiko did not permit herself to be tired. She pushed on, stopping only occasionally to take a bit of food. But she could not keep the pace of a sturdy peasant boy, so it was late afternoon before she came to what should have been a familiar stretch of road. The mountains rose from the plain to her right, and she could see near the river the familiar clump of woodlands where Fusa had brought her mushroom hunting in the fall. But past the woods where the village should have been there was no village. Her heartbeat quickened, for beyond the village where the farmhouse and smaller outbuildings of the estate had stood, there was nothing except a tiny shack on the land where the house had been. But Goro had told her it was gone. There was nothing to fear. Look, there on the hillside, the smoke rose from the pottery oven. And far off in the field nearest the river, a tiny bent form.

She began to run. "Mother! Fusa! I'm home."

The bent form straightened as she came near. "Goro! I'm here! Finally, I'm home!" The look on his face stopped her dead. *Why does he hate me?*

The dwarf bent his body in a bow so low that his long arms swept the ground he had been tilling. "I welcome you to my humble dwelling," he said, his voice heavy with sarcasm.

SIXTEEN
Waiting

She had said she was home, but she had been mistaken.
Nothing remained of home except the misshapen body
of the potter. Even his soul was gone. He spoke only
rarely, but his hatred of her flared in the narrow slit eyes.
The day after she came, he began to construct a mud hut
near the kiln, working night and day upon it. After it was
finished, he moved his wheel and his own meager possessions into it, leaving the shack to Takiko. Her bed was
a pile of rice straw without any covers, her only furniture
a tiny clay charcoal brazier. There were plenty of pottery
cups and bowls, but precious little to put into them. And
boasting the single quilt in either hut was the koto of
Goro's mother, jammed against the south wall.

Sometimes she wondered where the tears that had

flowed so freely the year before had gone. Why could she not weep for all those she loved who had died? Was it because their deaths seemed unreal? As though all those things had happened in some other lifetime? Despite Goro's anguished account, she could not picture her mother ugly and dying. She still expected her to return and take her in her arms, while those in little Emperor Antoku's court seemed but fantasies in a children's story.

As for Goro—what could she do? The man had turned monster. She would have fled his presence except that there was nowhere to flee. And—and there was Hideo's promise. She clung to this like an infant monkey to its mother's fur. In a few days he would come galloping down that road, and all would be well.

But May passed into June, and he did not come, and June turned into the rains of early summer and still he did not come. Her eyes were strained from peering down the road. She would go mad watching.

Goro was transplanting rice in the misting rain. The war was over. Why had the peasants not returned? She took off her straw sandals and rolled up the legs of her trousers. "Show me what to do," she demanded. "I want to work." He gave her a look that said she would never stick to such a task, but he did not send her away, so she bent over beside him and imitated as best she could the rhythm of his movements.

The fact that she knew he expected her to give up drove her all the more determinedly. She would not offer him the satisfaction, and though within the hour her back and legs were screaming out in pain, she clenched her teeth and kept doggedly on. By midafternoon the field swam about her in a dizzying pool, but she would not permit her body to faint or even to rest momentarily.

She concentrated on the coldness of the muddy water at her ankles.

Goro glanced at her from time to time out of the corner of his eye. *Good*, she thought, *good. I will show the little monkey I can be as stubborn as he is. I will show him.* Her pain passed into numbness, and the numbness into a kind of trance, but she kept going.

"It is done." Goro stood up abruptly. The rain that had started as a drizzle earlier was now beating steadily upon their bodies. Through her dreamlike state Takiko finally heard the meaning of the announcement. Slowly as though not to break her body in half, she brought herself to an upright position.

"You are tired," he said. "I will cook for both of us."

"Nonsense," she replied sharply. "I am a woman. I will cook."

After that day, though they seldom spoke, they worked together in the fields and ate together, what little there was to eat. Once the rice was transplanted, the vegetables had to be cultivated. Day after day she stood in the rain with a short hoe in her hand at war with every weed or blade of grass that dared invade the precious territory. For soon after the rains were over, they could expect fresh produce from these fields, and they coveted the life of every seed they had planted.

Some days when there seemed less to do in the fields, Goro would stump to his own hut and work with clay. And sometimes when she had finished her tasks, she would gently unwrap the koto and try to play. Her hands were thick with callouses and so stiff that they could not make the sounds her head commanded. But she practiced stubbornly. If she gave up, she would never be able to play again the way Hideo remembered. Her voice seemed hoarse and more like a crow's than a nightingale's but this, too, she would discipline until it regained its tone and color. She would permit nothing less.

The rains ceased, and the gray mud on the road to the northwest dried into hard gutters. Day after day she would climb barefoot the high paddles of the water-wheel and pump water from the river into the paddy fields. From her perch she could see far down the empty road. She tried not to watch it for the sight of a single horseman, but her eyes were weak and strayed in that direction despite her stern directions to herself. The rice grew tall, and the vegetables ripened. There was more than the two of them could eat or needed for winter store, so Goro took the surplus and some of his more common pots to the market in Otsu. He sold everything, and with his profit bought a quilt.

"Here," he grunted, handing it to her. She was torn between refusing it and accepting it, and in the end took it rather ungraciously. He did not seem to notice.

There were scarecrows in the rice fields now. Goro had fashioned them of straw and sticks. With the profits of a second vegetable sale he bought a new blouse and tore his old one to ribbons, which he tied to the scare-crows. The wind flapped the strips in the air and scat-tered all but the boldest birds.

Then one night in late summer he showed her a length of wood, which had come from the ruins of the house. "Until the rice is harvested, I become another scarecrow," he explained and went to sleep in the field.

She was awakened by screams. Hastily she pulled her trousers up over the blouse in which she slept and tied the sash as she ran out toward the noise. The moonlight was bright enough for her to see Goro struggling with another figure in the field. As she came closer she could tell that the other man had a short scythe which he sought to use as a weapon against the dwarf, but Goro was powerfully made and, grasping the man's arm, twisted until the blade dropped to the ground.

"Get the scythe," Goro commanded. Takiko bent forward and picked it up and then backed away. "Now, get back in the house," he commanded. "I've caught me a crow."

The captured man twisted, but Goro held fast, the stick of wood lifted high as a threat against escape.

"Why it's Fusa's nephew, Goro!"

"Yes, master"—it was a whine—"Don't you know me?"

"I know you for a thief."

"Please, for old times sake. I meant you no harm."

"Don't hurt him, Goro. He's Fusa's nephew. You remember him."

"Get into the house!" he roared, startling her into obedience.

She listened to the boy's screams as she sat huddled on her bed of straw against the cool mud wall. The noise sounded like a pig slaughtering on the farm in the old days. Would it never stop? She plugged her ears with her fingers, but she could still hear it. Goro was killing him—and for what? Because he was hungry. Did they not have enough rice to share with someone who had once worked these same fields? What kind of a monster had the man become? A coldness started in her chest and spread through her body.

Then it stopped. Once more she could hear the croaking of the frogs in the paddies. O merciful Kwannon, had he killed the boy? She strained for some further sound of the struggle, but all she could hear were the droning and croaking night sounds of summer. She wanted to go out, but fear of what she might see kept her motionless on the straw bed. At last she fell into a fitful sleep.

She was up, as usual, with the sun. She took her charcoal stove outside and lit the fire, looking about as she did for some clue as to the outcome of last night's happenings. No one was in the fields. At least no one was standing in the fields or lying where he might be seen. She felt wrapped in a clammy garment of dread. At last she spied Goro up at the kiln. He was making a fire in it. Had he planned to bake pottery today? Or—? She began to scream as she ran. "No! No! What have you done, you monster?"

Goro turned, the white-hot poker in his hand, a look of incredulity on his face.

"How could you?" She grabbed for the wooden handle of the poker.

"Fool!" Goro shouted. "Watch out!" But she stumbled and struck the bent end of the poker with her cheek.

"Takiko!"

"It's all right."

His eyes were bright with terror. She regained her footing and pulled herself up to a dignified posture. "I'm not hurt." At that moment the pain seared through her consciousness. *He has killed me, too,* she thought, and crumpled to the ground.

She was aware of the pain before she knew where she was or remembered what had happened. Goro had laid her on her bedding and covered her with her quilt. Something wet and cold was plastered on the bright line of pain cutting across her face. In a few moments she realized that it was tea leaves. The dwarf was somewhere nearby. She could hear his heavy breathing. No, that was her own breathing. If only she could faint again! The pain was too much to endure.

He was in the doorway. She could see the grotesque shadow of his body against the light. "I did not kill him," he said dully.

She tried to answer, but no sound came.

"Oh, Taki Chan—" It was a moan.

Did he expect her to bear his pain as well as her own? She turned her head to the wall and forced herself to repeat inside her head the words of every song she knew. It did not ease the pain, but it blunted its focus just a little. And it kept her from crying out. She would not cry out. Let her body explode first. She would not cry out.

The pain that could not be endured was endured, and with it the infection and the fever, until one morning she woke up and knew that she could get up, and so she did. Goro had soup bubbling on the charcoal burner in the yard before the house, and she dressed and joined him there. The brightness of the morning blinded her, and her cheek was tender as the sun beat upon it, but it seemed good to be outdoors. She sat down on her haunches beside the potter and took the bowl of soup he held out.

If Lady Chujo could only see me now. She smiled at the thought of Big Nose looking down at her crouched like a serf, with only crudely cut bamboo sticks to guide the bits of vegetables into her mouth from the soup bowl.

"You're feeling better."

"Umm." Even her language had deteriorated to the grunts of peasant speech.

"Kwannon be praised," the man said softly.

"I never knew you for a religious man, Goro."

"Then you know me well." He slurped his soup noisily. Over the rim of the bowl she caught his eyes looking at her. She smiled.

"Humph," he snorted, but his little eyes were smiling back.

They finished harvesting the rice together. The first few days she could feel the weakness of her body and cursed the days of idleness on her bed, but if Goro seemed to offer to let her rest, she shook him off. She would not give way to weakness now.

He made several trips to the market at Otsu and came back with quilts and clothes and utensils and a cart to pull food to market on. How wealthy they suddenly seemed! There was even dried fish for soup stock and sweet bean cakes for a harvest celebration.

She clucked over his extravagances like a thrifty farmwife while he grunted and pretended annoyance at all her nagging ways.

By fall a few of Goro's peasants came home from the wars. Goro sent them back to their wives' villages to collect what was left of their families after plague and famine, and assigned paddies and fields to each of them. The return of the peasants made no real change in their lives except that there were other human beings in sight again. The two of them worked as hard as ever, rethatching the roofs of their huts, drying fruits and vegetables for winter storage.

The road was not so empty now. Travelers passed along it from time to time, and still the sight of a horseman, or even a tall man on foot, had the power to quicken Takiko's pulse until he drew close enough to be clearly seen. But travelers brought word of the troubles in the capital. And there was good reason for Hideo's delay.

The Genji, having vanquished the Heike, now struggled for power among themselves. Yoritomo had attacked Yoshitsune's closest ally, and there was reason to believe that his next target would be his hero brother. One part of Takiko was torn with anxiety for Hideo, but the other rejoiced. Now she knew he was not delayed by choice. He would come when he could, just as he had promised her in the spring.

Winter came early, or perhaps it only seemed that way to Takiko after the southern winters on Yashima. Now when she did her laundry on the river bank, her hands cracked and bled from the icy water. She was glad for the quilts that Goro had splurged his money upon last summer and even took to borrowing the koto's wrapping on frosty nights.

It was harder for her to play the koto than ever. Her hands were painful, but she practiced every night, much to Goro's delight. One evening she was surprised to find him sitting outside her door in the cold night air. He pretended an errand, but she knew he had crept down from his own hut in order to hear the music better.

"If you spend the evening here, we save on oil and charcoal," she pointed out. It was all the invitation he needed. After supper he would stay for at least an hour, sometimes two, if she played longer, before stumping through the darkness to his own rough bed.

She was coming from the east field with a basket of turnips on her back when she saw the horseman. How had she ever deluded herself that the poor figures she had stared at coming up that road might be he? For when she saw him, it was beyond any doubt that it was he. He was not armored for battle, but he was gloriously dressed in a crimson outer garment and wore fur chaps on his legs. He was coming slowly, for he had a pack pony tied behind his war-horse. The larger beast pawed with impatience at the pace.

Her first impulse was to run, but shyness overcame her. Then he saw her and shouted in her direction, "Boy, come here!"

He thought her a boy. She smiled. How surprised he would be when he saw to whom he was yelling so rudely. She broke into a little trot.

"Yes, my lord." She looked up into his face.

"Goro the potter. Do you know him?"

"Yes, my lord." She was enjoying the game. It gave her time to collect her wits.

"Well?"

"Sir?" He thought her stupid. "Oh, this is his estate, sir."

The warrior looked at the huts scattered about the fields.

"The house was burned, sir." When would he recognize her? She could hardly keep from giggling.

"Are you his man?"

"No, sir." Slowly she reached up and took off the kerchief on her head. Then she untied her hair and shook it loose across her shoulders. She could feel the love rising from her heart and racing into her eyes as she looked up into his face.

He stared at her in silence. Then, disbelievingly, he said, "Takiko?"

"I have waited a long time."

She would never forget the change that came over his face. It was as though some hand had reached up from within his vitals and twisted his features. His stare traveled from her filthy straw-sandaled feet to her cracked and frostbitten hands to her dry and lusterless hair to her brown face cut in quarter by a streaked white scar. Her fingers flew to her cheek. She was not sure whether his eyes betrayed revulsion or fear.

"Our home is very humble, but you are welcome." The training of sixteen years came back. What wise god created etiquette as a haven for lost souls?

The warrior found his voice. "It has been a long time." He, too, fled into conventional manners as he slowly dismounted his prancing horse. "I wish I could stay, but . . . ."

"I understand." She dropped her eyes to her dirty feet.

"No," he said. "No, you don't."

"I know Yoshitsune is in trouble. He needs you more than I."

There was an awkward silence. "Yoshitsune has fled to Shikoku. I go to join Yoritomo."

"I see."

"When I come again in triumph. . . ."

Where had she heard this before? "Go in health, Hideo."

He swung himself once more into the saddle. "Bear yourself carefully until I return." But it was manners and not love that spoke. He spurred the already straining horse into a full gallop, dragging the poor terrified pack pony along behind, until they were only three dots far down the road.

"Farewell, Hideo," she whispered. "Farewell."

SEVENTEEN
To Change the Fragile Dream

She went to her hut and sat quietly in the darkness of the room. It was as though someone had jerked the tangled puzzle of her life into a single unknotted string.

Everything became clear: her birth—her life at Lady Uchinaka's, her father's death. The coming of her mother and herself to Goro's estate in Shiga—her fear and jealousy—the meeting with Hideo through Princess Aoi—going to court and into exile. Her traitorous love affair—her refusal to return with Goro—her cowardice in the face of death—her homecoming to Goro's bitterness and the accident. Now this. But this at last had made everything clear, and she knew what must be done to make recompense.

Goro did not speak to her of the warrior, though she

was sure he must know that Hideo had come—and gone. And though her own plans were made, she did not tell him of them, preferring to wait until all the winter's work, including preparations for a meager New Year's celebration, had been completed.

Two days before the New Year, everything was in readiness. She had scrubbed and washed and swept and cooked. It was time.

"I want to make a trip to the capital for the New Year," she said at breakfast.

He avoided her eyes. "Alone?" he asked.

"Yes."

"The road is not safe for a woman alone."

"No one takes me for a woman," she said with a half laugh.

"I do." He cleared his throat. "I have pottery for Kamaji." He spoke carefully without raising his eyes to her face. "Would it embarrass you to walk with me to the city?"

"Why should it embarrass me?" she asked sharply.

"Children laugh. . . ." His voice was that of an earnest child. "I am a very ugly person. . . ."

"So am I." She rose abruptly and began to clean up. "Can we leave at once?"

"If you will help me load the cart."

She brought one of her quilts out to where he was packing the pottery. "You can use this to wrap the better pieces," she offered. "And if I decide to stay for a few days . . . ."

"Yes, of course," he took it from her brusquely.

It was dark before they reached Gojo Bridge and the gates of the city were locked, so they huddled together under the quilt and pretended to sleep until dawn.

"I will go with you to Kamaji's," she said. "I want to visit the former Empress. Kamaji may have heard where she is."

"Yes," he agreed. "Kamaji is likely to know."

She could read the distress and questions in Kamaji's face when they met, but she gave him a steely stare, and the kind man said nothing. He responded to her inquiry that the former Empress had been permitted by Yoshi-tsune to enter a convent. She was reputed to be in the Jakko Temple, near the foot of Mount Hiei, north of the capital.

Now that her journey was nearing its end, Takiko was impatient to be off, and she went out of the shop and waited by the cart while Goro completed his trans-actions with the merchant. He came out at last, carrying two parcels, one wrapped in a kerchief, the other in straw matting, which he put down on the straw of the cart by her quilt.

"I'm off, Goro." She picked up the quilt. "Thank you for your kindness in bringing me this far along the way."

He ran his hand along the rough pole of the cart. "I want to go with you the rest of the way. It is a lonely wooded road."

She started to protest, but changed her mind. "Very well." She got beside him before the cart and took the other pole. Two oxen they were, and a strange yoking indeed.

"Won't you ride, Takiko?"

"No," she replied. "I'd rather pull with you."

They made their way out of the city toward the glowering face of Mount Hiei, a haven for wild beasts and warrior monks. The last day of 1185 was bitterly cold, and the first hour of their trip they fought against a sharp wind blowing off Lake Biwa into their faces. At length they reached the haven of the forest. The trees blocked both the wind and the pale winter sunshine.

From time to time they were aware of tiny, almost human eyes upon them and the chittering of the monkey inhabitants of the woods. The road now was hardly more than a footpath.

"Goro," she said, "I can find the way now. Why don't you return to the city before the gates are locked?"

"No. I would not let you travel alone on such a road." He pushed the cart into the underbrush and tied the parcels and quilt onto his back before they continued.

They stumbled onto the temple grounds as though by accident, for the small buildings were almost hidden by the forest growth and no attempt had been made to clear a garden. Takiko's first thought was that the pilgrimage had been in vain, for the broken roof tiles and shredded paper on the doors gave the appearance of abandonment. Her heart sank. But then she spotted a thin wisp of smoke coming from one of the tiny huts in the rear. They made their way through the tall grasses to this sign of life.

"Excuse me!" Takiko called at the doorway of the hut.

A small shaven head appeared. For a moment the two of them stared at each other in the shadowed light of the forest.

"Your Majesty." Takiko dropped to her knees and prostrated herself upon the ground.

"It is Takiko, isn't it?" Kenreimon'in helped the girl to her feet. "You are very welcome, my child."

Goro had dropped to his knees a few feet behind her and waited there. She turned to him. "I will stay here for a while, Goro. Thank you for your kindness along the way."

"It was nothing," he murmured without moving.

"If you do not hurry," she said gently, "the city gates will be locked."

"Yes," he said absently. There was a silence. At last he got to his short legs and swung the parcels wrapped in her quilt from his back. "The straw-wrapped one is an offering. I thought you might want something for an offering."

"You were thoughtful."

"The other is for you—a New Year's token."

She smiled her thanks. "Go in health, Goro."

He bowed his funny little bow with his long arms sweeping the ground. When he raised his head, she could see that his monkey eyes were strangely bright. Without another word he turned and stumped off quickly out of sight.

After a meager meal of bean curd and root tea, Takiko was taken to the tumbledown temple for prayers with the nuns. There were scarcely a dozen of them, and all of them, even Kenreimon'in, were dressed in motley garments of cotton and silk mixed. The glory of her people had come to this wilderness and to this despair. But at least Takiko was with the other Heike women now. She could begin to repay the debt of her self-pride and whatever sins of her former lives that had brought her family and her clan to ruin.

To the Empress that afternoon Takiko made full confession and begged that despite her unworthiness she be allowed to enter the convent as a novice and give what was left of her life to making amends. Tomorrow a New Year would open and with it a new life.

"You are sure this is what you must do, little Takiko?" Kenreimon'in's eyes were on the girl's long hair.

"Yes, your Holiness."

"Life here is hard." There was no self-pity in her voice.

"Life is hard everywhere."

The Empress looked tenderly into Takiko's brown, scarred face. "Yes," she said.

"I—Goro gave me an offering for the temple." She pushed forward the straw-wrapped parcel.

"And the other?"

She blushed despite herself. "He said it was a New Year's token for me."

The Empress smiled. "First your gift—then Buddha's."

Takiko fumbled at the kerchief knots. Inside was a silk garment. In the dim light it seemed almost white, but it was in fact a sky-breath blue with tiny birds embroidered upon it in a slightly deeper blue. The old fool, it must have taken every copper of his profits.

Kenreimon'in's shaven head was bowed. Without realizing it, her eyes had dropped to look at her own patch-quilt of a garment. She caught herself. "Very lovely," she smiled.

"Now for Buddha." Suddenly Takiko knew what the gift in the straw wrapping must be. She could hardly control the shaking of her hands as she opened the parcel.

Yes. It was the crooked cup from Kamaji's shelf. She set the lid in place.

The Empress picked it up, and with the practiced eye of an educated woman of the court, examined the strange piece from every angle. Then she put it down before her. She made no move to lift the lid.

Takiko could not restrain herself. "Inside," she said, "inside the lid, it is very beautiful."

The Empress shook her head. "It is not possible that the inside could be lovelier than this," she replied, regarding the crooked shape and strange glazing with shining eyes. Her hands were in an attitude of prayer.

"So," she said at last, "you want to give your life to prayer and poverty."

The girl nodded. "Yes, your Holiness."

Now Kenreimon'in lifted the lid of the teacup and slowly traced the form of the bird with the tip of her finger. Carefully she replaced the lid and raised her eyes to meet Takiko's. "You have the right, my child, to give up your life. Indeed, perhaps it is your duty to do so. But"—her eyes rested again upon the crooked cup—"I wonder if this is the place."

"Madam!"

"I cannot remember, Taki Chan, that you were ever too eager to pray." She smiled to soften the words.

Takiko's tanned face flushed a deep reddish brown. *Don't turn me away!* She pleaded silently.

"I have been thinking," the Empress continued, "about our nation. It lies wounded, Takiko. Perhaps the wound is mortal. I pray not. But where do we turn for healing? I have learned what my father never knew, that the power of armies can only destroy." She stroked the crooked cup with her forefinger. "Do you remember how my mother used to say that your music was better for my son than medicine? Perhaps, Takiko, we are meant to learn that beauty can heal."

"I have learned, madam, that beauty is a mockery." Takiko's voice was hardly more than a whisper.

"Yes," answered the gentle voice. "I have been mocked by beauty, too. But it was the beauty which cost me nothing that in the end turned upon me." She was quiet, staring at the cup as though breathing strength from it. Then she put her hand on Takiko's cracked and calloused one. "If your music had healing power when you were a vain and thoughtless child, what might it accomplish now?"

"Oh, madam, even if you are right—even if the music can heal—you are all gone. There is no one left to listen now but peasants—and Goro."

"Is that the little god's name?"

Takiko snatched off her straw sandals and hung them over her arm, so they would not hinder her as she scrambled down the mountain path. Goro was slower than she, and he had the cart to pull. If she ran, she could catch up to him before he got to the city gates. They would travel all night and just as the morning of the New Year broke, they would be home. She would make him soup with rice dumplings, and when he had drunk it, she would say: "Goro, I have been thinking that you should marry again. Now there is no one but me to help you in the fields or with the pottery. You don't even have an heir. A man like you needs to have many sons. If you marry someone else, I will have no place to go. Besides, we are used to each other. I am strong and at a good age for child-bearing. It is only sensible that we should marry."

She tried to picture his reaction. He was more than likely to object—he was too old—too poor—too ugly. Goro was a stubborn man, but in the end she could persuade him. And then—and then for the rest of his life she would serve him—prepare his food, till his fields, fire his kiln, warm his bed, bear him a dozen beautiful children, play her koto and sing, and heal all the terrible wounds on his torn and battered soul.

When she turned the curve near the place where they had left the cart, she saw him sitting on the ground with his wide back to the path. She crept up behind him and, like a child, put her hands over his eyes.

He grasped her wrists in his big hands. "Are you a phantom sent to taunt me?" he whispered.

"No, Goro. It's me, Takiko."

He turned, revealing a face so anguished that suddenly all Takiko's plans and playfulness dissolved into weeping. She could not control it.

Goro moved to her side. "There, there," he patted her head. "There, Taki Chan. You musn't waste your tears on a crazy old dwarf. You know me. I'll be all right. Don't worry."

"I'm not worrying about you," she sobbed. "I just want you to take me with you."

His big hand rested gently on her hair. "Well," he said finally. "Well, then, if you will stop crying and help me with this cart, we can be on our way." He got to his feet. "With luck we can drink our New Year's soup at home."

The daughter of a samurai does not cry out in childbirth. Within her head Takiko laughed at the injunction. It was as though her very body was the koto of a god whose powerful hand struck a chord so fierce that for the wild moment she became the storm music of the sea. Then throbbing, ebbing, the great wave would pass over her, and she would drift on the surface of the water, the sun warm upon her face until another stroke upon the strings.

I am mixing it all up. She smiled. *I am music and storm and strings. I am Izanami as She brooded over Creation.*

The storm built with a deafening crescendo until her flesh could no longer contain it. Takiko cried out—a cry of triumph and joy. Who could keep silent at such a victory?

Then she heard a tiny angry squall.

"It is a girl," the peasant midwife observed dully.

Goro stumped across the small room to where his wife and baby lay and knelt beside the quilts.

"It is only a girl," Takiko confessed, worshiping the thatch of black hair which lay upon her breast.

Goro put his big hand across the body of the child and with one brown finger traced the scar on Takiko's cheek. "Isn't that what you are, Taki Chan—a mere girl child?"

She nodded, her throat too full for speech.

Goro shook his head. "I'm no match for two of you— a little man like me."

"Oh, you sly little man. You know you will have won her over to yourself before she's weaned."

Then they laughed and wept together without caring if the peasants outside the hut were listening or not.